Chapter One

You would not want to meet a Sea Witch. They had pale green skin, were very thin, and gaunt with long frizzy hair. They dressed in black dresses which – it was said – were made of the skin of their enemies; nothing was safe from the witches.

Their almond-shaped eyes were long black slits with yellow pupils. Their hands were huge black claws matched with extremely big feet for their small frames. The size of their feet was quite useful. It gave them the momentum to speed their broomsticks along through the sky.

They could fly on land, and underwater. They were enemies to all marine life. The Sea Witches could change shape from a mouse to a horse at lightning speed. Sea Witches tended to travel in groups, usually on the lookout for children – a favourite delicacy. The younger the better, as they were more tender. They did not tend to eat the adults as they were rather tough, and the meat tended to lodge in between their teeth. These they kept as slaves.

Stevie Rump was twelve years old when his parents were abducted by Sea Witches.

The Caribbean Island where he lived had been a safe haven for a long time, but since the Sea Witches had won the final battle in the War of the Mermaids, the Sea Witches now ruled the sea, and everyone was in fear of them. Even the frightening one-eyed monsters, the Eperviers, obeyed their every command. These huge lumbering hawk-headed creatures guarded the white marble gates leading to the spiralling black tower where the witches lived.

The witches cackled in contempt of the law when slavery was abolished in the Caribbean two years before they kidnapped Stevie's parents. Their arrogance, and the lack of any one strong enough to stop them meant they did exactly as they pleased.

They had their followers: Warlocks and the fearsome Dog Pirates were in league with them.

One day the Sea Witches came where Stevie lived with his parents, who were teaching in the old missionary hut in Soufriere, St Lucia. The Sea Witches rounded up all the children and teachers and took them away in a big black pirate ship. That was the last anyone saw of them.

Stevie had been unwell with a heavy cold which began to get worse in the classroom. His parents had told him to go back to the house, stay out of the sun, and rest in the house rather than pass it on to the other children. He would not be on his own as Winnie, who helped out in the house, would be there.

But Stevie had not gone back to the house. Instead, he had gone to fish in a stream, away from the house so he could not be seen. He was determined to beat his friend Robert in Soufriere's Annual Fishing competition.

Robert had beaten him twice. Stevie felt that this time, with more practice, and effort, he would beat him. Time had gone by. He had not meant to stay out so long. He hoped Winnie would not be looking for him, and that his parents had not come back to check on him. If his parents assumed he had stayed in the house and had not gone up to speak to Winnie, he knew he would be okay. If, however, they came back to the house, he would be in deep trouble and there would be no more fishing trips.

His cold had been just a minor one. Stevie embellished it to make it seem worse than it was, something he had never done before. But fishing was all he had on his mind. He was sick of Robert and his jibes about hammering him into the ground.

It had been a very hot day, a day not made easier with the sun beating down on him when he was fishing. He had nearly caught a Marlin, but just as he attempted to net it, it had twisted its body round, and escaped. Fed up because he had caught nothing, he decided to go back to the house. It was hotter than normal. Sweat poured off him. Staggering up the hill, the mild cold now seemed much worse. As he came up the hill to the house, it was eerily quiet. Too quiet.

Out of nowhere, smoky black billowing clouds poured down the hill towards him in bursts. The smoke filled his lungs, making him choke, and his eyes water. More smoke came down the hill. He raced up the hill as fast as he could. From the front of the house he could see pieces of family furniture that had been dragged outside. Even the kitchen table was lying face down on the ground. It was as if the house had been pulled apart. Precious china had been smashed, and their photos damaged. The luscious fruit on the trees were singed black. The brightly-coloured parrots that usually filled the trees had flown away.

Stevie shouted for Winnie. She was nowhere to be seen. He raced round the back of the house. He could not see her. He then ran towards the schoolhouse, half falling as he ran. It had been burnt down. Looking desperately for his parents he could not find them. What had happened? Where were his parents?

A slight movement made him half turn, but he was stopped in his tracks. Hook-like claws grabbed him by the neck, half choking him. Unable to free his neck he was dragged along the ground. There was a strong smell of seaweed on whatever was holding him. Terrified, he once again tried to wriggle out of the creature's grasp, but it was too strong. What was it?

Whatever had him was now travelling at full speed. His feet scraped along the ground, making tram lines in their wake. It seemed to have super-human strength.

"Get away from him!" a booming voice shouted.

The grip on Stevie was released and he fell to the ground, scrambling to get away from whatever had been holding him.

He looked up into the face of a snarling Sea Witch.

But she was looking behind him. Her green face contorted as she screeched, "Walk away and leave me with the boy. Otherwise, you will be taken and we will destroy you and your home once and for all."

The voice that answered back had a strong Caribbean accent, "I don't think so. You have taken what you need. Leave the boy and go."

The witch gave a false laugh replying "I want the boy. I will take him and you will die."

With that, sparks flashed over Stevie's head as he crawled away from the fight. The witch aimed her wand at his rescuer. They followed suit with their own wand. The witch went flying through the air. As she tried to get up, she was thrown back in the air, her long red hair falling in dry rat's tails down her back. His rescuer then aimed their wand once again at the witch. A blue lined formed round the witch. She tried to get past it but it stopped her. She was firmly stuck behind it.

Stevie got to his feet.

"Are you alright, boy?" asked his rescuer.

He found himself looking into the eyes of a small dark skinned woman with coloured hair. Her dark brown eyes showed concern. Managing to mouth, "Yes" he rubbed his aching neck. They both looked at the trapped witch.

"Do not worry about her," the woman spoke. "I will deal with her."

With that and a few chants of her wand, the witch went screaming high up into the sky.

"She has gone to a place where she will not trouble you again," came the voice full of mirth. "My name is Andrina. I will not hurt you. Who are you? Who is it you are looking for?"

He replied, "My name is Stevie Rump. My parents teach in the school hut. They are gone. So are all my school friends." Trying to speak further, he could only gulp through his tears.

"The Sea Witches have taken them," said Andrina.
"Why?" asked Stevie.

"They take them as slaves."

"Can you help me find them?"

"No, I can't Stevie. I am trapped on this island. The last time the witches came here they placed a spell on me. I can never leave here. Do you have any other family on the Island?" The grim reality of his situation hit Stevie and he mumbled, "No," tears streamed down his face.

"Well, Stevie, I think you should come with me. I hope you are good at climbing. It is very steep where I live." With that she took his hand, smiled at him, and they started walking.

Chapter Two

The route to Andrina's home was long, and winding, and a sheer drop if you had the misfortune to fall. The green hills turned into grey rocks that were tricky climbing. Stevie kept looking ahead, trying not to look down, and saw that it had become mountainous.

Andrina walked barefoot, and the rocks did not appear to hurt her feet.

As she walked, she told Stevie she had seen the smoke when she was delivering eye ointment to a farmer. She came down to investigate to see if she could help.

"I knew what had happened. It happens all the time. After the Sea Witches won the battle against the Mermaids, no-one has been able to defeat them. Even the British and French turn a blind eye and let them do as they like," she said sadly.

"Will they come back and get us?" asked Stevie.

"No," she replied. "They have all they need at the moment. Come on, keep walking. There is not much further to go."

They passed remote farms all well off the beaten track. Looking into Stevie's large hazel eyes Andrina felt his grief.

Her sister, Lucella, had been taken by the Sea Witches years ago.

Putting her arm round his shoulder, she led him to her strange little house. It was near a volcano, most people thought she was mad to live up here, but it suited her. No-one ever passed this way.

She lived at the very top of the west side of the island. The witches had only taken people from the bottom of the island, too lazy to collect the others further up the hills.

Andrina's home was a pink crumbling sandstone house with the front wooden door painted a dark pink. The house leaned to one side, and when the wind blew it appeared to move and you really thought a strong gust would blow the house over.

The garden was surrounded by scented fruit trees and mango, breadfruit, and coconut trees lined the path to her house. Volcanic rock, and ash filled the garden, covering it in a white film, which had herbs growing out of it.

Andrina had a thin walnut-brown face that was heavilylined, with sharp eyes, and a small snub nose.

Her hair was amazing! It was multi-coloured. The blazing sun had bleached the natural auburn to part-white, and partblue, which matched her personality.

She had tried to get the original colour back with the help of her magic wand, but never seemed to get it right. She wore her hair in a thick bun and her clothes were brightly-coloured cottons.

Inside, the house was crammed with potions, and gailycoloured jars. The kitchen cupboards were filled with them. She was known as the local healer. Locals came to her for all matter of ailments.

Andrina was half-human, half-witch, and she had travelled all over the world on her broomstick. She had even taught the little white mice that lived in her garden to talk. It was fun listening to them at night, however, it's a different story when you could hear them arguing. More than once Stevie had had to get up and ask them to keep the noise down so he could get some sleep.

It was certainly an eccentric place to live in. You would get up for breakfast and a bat or parrot would whiz past your head.

Andrina could make marvellous cakes. For his birthday she made a huge chocolate cake with a brown and yellow spider made of marzipan sitting in an intricate white sugar-crafted web.

When Stevie blew out the candles, the spider appeared to run along the web towards him. It was so life-like.

But even on that day, he thought of his parents and wondered if they were still alive.

Stevie became very fond of Andrina, but as the days went by, the yearning to find his parents grew stronger.

Andrina also had her share of heartbreak. After they had taken her sister, the witches had plagued the rest of her family.

Her family finally left the island out of fear, and Andrina moved up near the volcano for safety. It was only then that the Sea Witches finally left her in peace.

Stevie was a bright boy, but Andrina's books were limited. There was now no school on the island and she could not trust anyone to take him to another of the island schools. Many of the locals, out of fear, acted as spies for the witches. But Stevie had other plans.

After a month of living with Andrina, Stevie decided he would look for his parents. There was a sailing ship called *The Black Scorpion* going out to sea, and they needed a cabin boy.

Stevie thought if he got this job he might find out what happened to his parents.

Andrina tried to persuade him to stay, telling to wait until he was older, but he would not listen. He secured the job as cabin boy, and within a month he was leaving the little house to set sail on the Caribbean Sea.

Frightened, but excited at the same time, he listened to Andrina's advice as she was seeing him off. She warned him it would be a tough, that he should only speak when spoken to, and if anything went wrong to come back - there would always be a home with her. She then waved goodbye to the lanky, blonde- haired boy.

Chapter Three

Stevie did not have it easy on the ship. With a surname like Rump he was, to coin the phrase, 'the butt of many jokes'.

After he had lost his last fight, he realised it wasn't worth a bloody nose or a ripped shirt. The tormentors soon became bored when they realised they could not goad him any further. Rump was a horrible surname, but he was stuck with it. So that was that. He just wished they wouldn't call him Rump instead of Stevie. But it amused the crew to call him by his surname.

Besides, he was more concerned with the Captain of the ship, a large black Labrador called Captain Casson. He could be hard on his crew. Often Stevie would hear the screams of some unfortunate as they were given thirty lashes, usually for some minor offence.

He had been shouted at by the Captain for not polishing his shoes well enough even when they gleamed and you could see your face in them. So, he had taken Andrina's advice and learnt to keep his head down, especially when the Captain was angry. He was a strong-minded boy, but he knew this was not forever.

Bruce, the ship's cook, was his best friend. They were a double act. Bruce had found out the main cargo was going to

Jack Island. It wasn't tea and coffee. It was pearls. This believed to be plunder the witches had taken from other ships.

The Captain, was, he had found out, a friend of the Sea Witches. Stevie felt there were few people on board the ship he could trust. He had shown a photo of his parents to Bruce.

Bruce related to him. He had not had an easy life. When he had been a kitten, both he and his auntie had been thrown into a bag that was sealed up, and left on the roadside by cruel owners. Fortunately, they managed to escape.

Then, his Auntie had been taken by Sea Witches, and Bruce had been left to fend for himself.

He was now a great friend to Stevie, but his habits left a lot to be desired. Catching, and killing rats on the ship, he would then have them as a lunch time snack, which made Stevie's stomach turn. Also, as a cook, Bruce had a rough, and tumble way of cooking, having somewhat unhygienic habits with cat hair often swimming in the soup. But no-one appeared to be bothered. The food always tasted really good.

Then, odd things started to happen on board the ship. Kegs of rum went missing. Fishing nets had been found cut. It was believed to be the work of the Sea Witches.

It was a frightening thought. The crew were terrified of the witches, who were referred to by mariners as 'Cocaya', a spirit which feasts on humans.

There were tales of these spirits plucking the eyes out of mariners, and leaving them for the crows to finish off.

Little bundles of sticks had been found lying outside the Captain's cabin, but he refused to listen to their fears. Why would they come on board his ship? He had nothing to fear, he thought.

What the crew didn't know was that he acted as a spy for the witches. Travelling through the Caribbean Islands, he would find out information about the people living there. It was then easy for the Sea Witches to round the islanders up and take them as slaves.

But he was double-crossing the Sea Witches, and had stolen jewellery from some of those captured. He thought he was quite safe, so he refused to listen to their 'superstitious nonsense' and ordered the crew back to work.

A lone albatross kept circling the ship…an ill omen. There were black clouds in the sky and the sea had become turbulent.

The usual shoal of dolphins had stopped following in the ship's wake. Even the friendly mermaids and sea horses had kept nervously away.

Terrified, the only time the crew spoke about it was quietly to each other late at night. This was after the Captain had fired a pistol in the air and ordered no further gossip. It was only the other day he had thrown the cabin puppy into the shark infested waters for spilling salt on him while serving. Luckily, the puppy had been rescued by mermaids and taken to another island where it was looked after by a family of greyhounds.

It was in the early hours of the morning that all hell was let loose. The Captain ran from his cabin firing his pistol at what appeared to be some invisible presence. He screamed that fiends were after him. There was nothing there.

Then what appeared to be black shadows crawled from the sea into the ship. They gradually took shape, turning into canine form. They were pirates. The Dog Pirates.

They charged at the crew plunging their swords into the unfortunate wretches, and throwing them into the sea. But worse was to come. Great White sharks, Hammerheads, and Eagle Rays arrived to finish the crew off.

The Captain, seeing this, tried to hide but was caught by one of the Dog Pirates and thrown into the water, too. Within minutes all you could see was his hat bobbing on the sea.

Nothing else remained of him. It seemed the sharks had made a good meal of him.

Stevie, finding a chance in all the commotion hid between the barrels of rum. Frightened to even breathe. His legs were like jelly. He really wanted to scratch his nose but daren't.

The pirates then rounded up the rest of the crew who surrendered to them. Stevie was lucky there were so many barrels on deck, or he would have been seen straightaway.

It was then that he heard a loud baritone voice. The voice became louder. He could make out what seemed to be a South African accent, the vowels deeply accentuated. What he didn't know was that this was Ethan, a notorious Rhodesian Ridgeback Pirate.

Stevie had heard about him, and that Ethan kept the skulls of his enemies as trophies, and that he had never lost a battle. Ethan was known in the Caribbean as one of the most deadly pirates.

Stevie peeped out from his hiding place to see where the voice was coming from.

With Ethan were his second in command officers, 'The McCarthy Twins'. Two pure white pit bull terriers. They had joined up with Ethan in St Lucia, when town folk had tried to hang them after they killed the Mayor. They were friends of Gledwyn, Stevie had been told.

Gledwyn the Witch lived on the Island of Glendowwer. She was believed to be a cruel, evil witch. People were frightened to speak her name. It was even said she drank human blood. She lived in a huge black spiralling tower that rose ominously from the sea. She was believed to live with her mother and daughter, and one of the crew had told Stevie that the spirit of Gledwyn's grandmother haunted the tower. Her wailing shrieks could be heard way out to sea and put a cold fear in the hearts of mariners out in their fishing boats at night.

The father of Larissa, daughter of Gledwyn, had been a gigantic natter jack toad. He was killed in the War of the Mermaids. It had been a bloody fight, but the witches had finally won. Gledwyn, in a violent rage, swore revenge on all mermaids and sea creatures. They had paid dearly for her husband's death.

Chapter Four

Stevie was getting very uncomfortable in his hiding place, becoming very hot, and dying for something to drink. He felt a dry cough coming up so he held his fist tightly against his mouth to try and smother any sound coming out. But there was worse to come.

Something was tickling his foot. The urge to giggle was unbearable. He could hardly breathe. The deck was getting red hot from the sun. His foot was being tickled even more.

A shrill high-pitched voice suddenly spoke out saying, "What have we here?"

Stevie had to hold his head because the high decibels of the voice caused his head to burn inside. The pain was unbearable.

"Look!" shouted the voice again.

Then in almost a whisper, "A boy. My favourite food. Such soft tender skin. Nice and golden. Half-cooked and ready for me to eat," it hissed gleefully.

Stevie could now see a dark shadow engulfing him. Looking up he peered into the eyes of a giant brown python. It twisted its body round his waist, and dragged him out from behind the barrels. This action made a dozen casks roll down the deck. The snake then released him and he fell to the ground.

It then rose up to full height, and started swaying in front of him. Stevie started to feel tired. He could hardly keep his eyes open. Wanting to go and lie down. Now beyond the point of terror, any minute he expected to be the snake's early breakfast. With his eyes half-open he could see into the snake's great mouth. It was like a huge cavern. Spit oozed off its chin. Its mouth was stretching wider and wider. The snake's eyes were red and slanted. Stevie willed himself to stay awake, counting numbers in his head. There was nowhere to escape. Where he had been thrown was an open space on deck. He closed his eyes, expecting now to be the snake's lunch and hoping his death would be quick.

"What the hell do you think you are doing?" the snake screamed out.

Stevie opened his eyes wide. There was a large shape. He was unable to make it out because of the steamy breath of the snake obscuring it. There was a scuffle. The snake appeared to be shrinking away from him. The mass he could not make out at first was now visible. It was Ethan the Dog Pirate.

He picked up the snake, coiled it up, and had it screaming, and hissing under his arm. The snake, defeated, begged to be released. The Ridgeback released its grip.

"If you leave the boy alone, I will release you. He may be useful to me for bartering with. He would be a disappointing meal. He is too thin. Forget him. There will be plenty more children you can eat later."

The snake started whining, "Give me back my snack…I want my snack."

It continued whining, but the Ridgeback would not give in to it. The snake was let go and it slithered along the deck.

At a safe distance it turned round and screeched, "Don't ever do that again, Ethan. I will let this one go, but if you ever do that again you will regret it." It moved further away.

The Ridgeback laughed showing large pointy teeth.

"You need me so don't waste your threats on me. When do we pick up the cargo?"

The snake replied, "Not long now. But if we are late she will not be happy."

"That is not a problem we will be on time, but you had better make sure the cargo is intact and there is nothing missing."

The snake replied sulkily, "I won't."

It must be Gledwyn they were talking about, thought Stevie. The cargo the snake mentioned…were they talking about kidnapped people? That would be Jack Island.

A gut feeling told Stevie his parents were at Glendowwer. Gledwyn would not be at the tower with only her daughter and mother; there would be her followers, and witches and warlocks there. He knew he would have to get people to help him rescue his parents. The many stories he had heard of people trying to escape from Glendowwer had been grim. They had been recaptured and tied to the rocks, left to die for the Eperviers to eat.

Bruce had even told him about zombies living there. They had been shipwrecked people. The witches had kept their souls in caskets so they could never escape. They were doomed to obey the witches' every command.

The snake, now apparently bored with the conversation with the Ridgeback, slithered over and silently dropped into the sea.

The Ridgeback, remembering Stevie, picked him up and threw him over its back. The dog carried him into a small cabin and threw him on a pile of sack cloth on the bed.

Growling at him menacingly it said, "Keep quiet and don't try and escape. There is no way out. I would be very angry if you did try to escape. I would let the snake eat you. It would be a very painful way to die. Do you understand?"

Stevie nodded and the Ridgeback went out the door of the cabin.

Stevie lay on the bed and gave a sigh of relief. Alone now, but he was very thirsty. His lips felt dry, and he was hungry.

The image of the snake was terrifying. Being eaten by a snake would, he imagined, be a painful way to die, as the Ridgeback had said.

Looking out the porthole window, the strong wind had made the sea water rise tenfold. The water was rising. He would be noticed if he attempted to steal a small boat and escape.

He thought about Bruce and hoped nothing had happened to him, and that the Dog Pirates had not hurt him. Bruce was a good cook, so surely they would keep him. But, he was a cat.

A rap on the door brought him out of his wonderings. The door opened and it was Bruce.

"I was just thinking about you!" said Stevie. Relieved he was not hurt. Stevie picked his dumpy pal up and hugged him.

"Gerroff!" shouted Bruce although secretly pleased. A slight purr started coming from Bruce. He could not stop it. It then developed into hiccups. It made Stevie laugh.

When the hiccups subsided, Stevie asked Bruce, "Why did they not throw you overboard? I thought dogs hated cats."

"I think," answered Bruce, "they spared me because of my cooking ability." He said modestly scratching his flea-bitten ear. "I was cooking Kingfish soup when they came into the kitchen. A huge black Rottweiler called Saros liked it and started eating it.

"Bruce, you are going to have to make them even happier with other dishes," Stevie said.

"I know, but I do have a secret weapon which I will reveal to you later," said Bruce mysteriously.

"Oh, I nearly forgot. Here, have some food."

Bruce produced out of the pocket of his chef's apron a squashed pork sandwich. Stevie hungrily wolfed it down.
Bruce then passed him a small bottle of water.

"Thanks," said Stevie in between gulps.

As Stevie was drinking the water, Bruce produced a piece of brown tobacco and started to chew on it.

"Bruce that is disgusting. Why do you eat that? It's foul. It will make your teeth black."

Bruce ignored him, and continued to chew as Stevie spoke saying, "Did you see the giant snake that came on to the ship?

I have never been so frightened. I really thought it was going to swallow me up."

"I'm not surprised. Did you know it was a Sea Witch? They can change shape." said Bruce now chomping very loudly. "You are lucky to be alive. They swallow their prey whole, and you're then crushed to death inside their mouths." "Yuk," said Stevie shivering at the thought.

"Where do these witches come from?" asked Stevie.

"They live in the caverns of the sea. It's they who are responsible for shipwrecks round here," said Bruce. "I hear they eat mer children. It's their favourite food. What a disappointment you would have been to the snake. All skin and bones."

"I wonder why Ethan didn't let the snake eat me" said Stevie.

"It is odd. He is ruthless. Maybe he thinks he will get more money if he sells you to the witches. I heard he spies for Gledwyn and sells slaves to her. Stevie, do as the pirates say. I will put a word in with Saros and ask if you can help me in the kitchen. We will have to think of a way of escaping, but we need time to think about it. I'm going to have to go. I've got to get this evening meal ready. I have to show them they need me.

I'm going to have to do a magnificent spread. If I don't they might throw me to the sharks."

Bruce looked worried and Stevie was saddened by this.

"Don't worry, Bruce. I'm sure you will come up trumps," said Stevie reassuringly.

"Oh, I'll be alright. I always come up trumps," he said putting on a brace face and patting Stevie's shoulder. He then went out the door.

Stevie went back to the bed and flopped down on his back. He put his hands behind his head and sighed to himself, wondering how he and Bruce were going to get off the ship. Still thinking about the snake, he nodded off and was woken up by rough hands shaking him. The room was now dark. He must have been asleep a long time.

"Wake up you," said a gruff voice. A white pit bull terrier shook him.

Stevie quickly got up.

"Come with me."

Walking with the pit bull, Stevie kept quiet. It had a meanlooking face - not an animal to be messed with.

Stevie followed the dog into the dining room, where Ethan was seated at the head of the table. Glancing up as he came in the door and looking slightly annoyed, Ethan said to Stevie,

"You are going to eat with us boy. What is your name?"

"Stevie Rump, Sir."

A titter of laughter went round the table but was swiftly stopped with a look from Ethan.

Turning to Stevie he said, "Help yourself to the food."

He muttered a thank you, sat down and kept his head down. However, curiosity got the better of him and he looked around the table.

To his right was a bow-legged Cairn terrier struggling with plates of food. Stevie took some off him and placed them on the table. The food on the table was an amazing sight. How had Bruce pulled this off?

There were serving dishes filled with creamy goat curry, scented rice, and husks of bread. Chicken wings in spicy sauces, roast potatoes, and vegetables. There were also slabs of plain cakes covered in coconut icing.

"Eat," commanded Ethan.

Stevie looked in astonishment as more food arrived: huge hams, fried eggs, and tropical fruit. He tucked in, enjoying every mouthful. Then he had a look around the table.

Across the table was a Doberman called Blake. He had a broad Caribbean accent, and didn't eat much, preferring to drink his rum.

At his side was a liver, and white spaniel called Toby. The exact opposite of Blake, he ate three cakes in one go. His watery brown eyes never left the group, agreeing with everything being said. He had a nauseating whiny voice which started to get on Stevie's nerves. Stevie avoided catching his eye as he felt he could be trouble.

Next to Toby was an enormous Rottweiler called Saros. He was a big black muscular dog with small almond shaped eyes. The fur on his face was inky black and smooth .His head was twice the size of Stevie's. When he spoke his pointed teeth met at a huge scissor shaped point. His grey shirt had ridden up his black and brown chest. One of his parents had been an Italian mastiff, hence his size. No-one messed with him. The scars on his forehead told a tale. On one of his forearms was tattoo of a skull. His table manners were disgusting, and he talked with food spilling out of his mouth. When he ate, he made loud gulping noises. If Stevie had not been so hungry, he would have been put off his food.

Saros, sensing Stevie was watching him, threw a large piece of bread at him. It hit Stevie full on the forehead. The Rottweiler, pleased with his aim, rolled back his head and laughed and laughed, then banged his fist on the table with dinner plate-size paws. This action sent some of the contents of the food off the table. Saros would have continued doing this if Ethan had not shouted at him to stop. To Stevie's surprise Saros immediately stopped.

Stevie could understand why, after looking at the demonic look in Ethan's slanted golden eyes. Ethan was not as large as Saros, but he was still a very muscular dog. His short ears would flap up if he was listening to anything of interest. He had what looked like a small mask of black fur covering his eyes and nose, a wheaten coloured coat with small white circles on his chest, and a long curved tail. As usual, he wore the trademark brown waistcoat and leather boots. Unlike all the other pirates, Ethan had very good table manners.

Stevie's parents had told him the history of the Dog Pirates. A hundred years ago they had lived on the Island of Bonay, which was not far off St Kitts. They had lived there quite peacefully, until the English invaded the island, taking dogs as slaves. The homes of those left behind were then burned. Anything of value had been taken. But they hadn't counted on the dogs being escape artists.

The dogs, vengeful, had united with the Sea Witches to capture the humans, using them as slaves instead.

Stevie continued looking round the table. There was a beagle with a lisp, followed by the McCarthy Twins - two pure white

Pit Bull Terriers with pink round eyes. Their snouts were raspberry pink and small black moles covered their faces. Both dogs had round black patches round one of their eyes. They wore black vests, and around their waists were glistening swords. On the end of their white paws were long red curled nails. These, they sometimes used as daggers to attack their enemies. They didn't say much. Just having the effect of looking menacing was enough.

Stevie had managed to pick up some parts of Ethan's conversation with Saros. The next cargo pickup would be the next evening. Ethan noticing Stevie showing interest in what he was saying to Saros and said he could now go back to his room. He did as he was told and fell fast asleep on his tiny bed.

Tomorrow, if he had a chance to see Bruce, they would have to put their heads together and think of an escape plan.

"But why had they fed him so well?"

Was it because he was too skinny and Gledwyn liked plump children? He ended up having a very restless night with dreams turning into nightmares.

Chapter Five

The next morning Stevie was given the job of peeling the potatoes and carrots in the kitchen. This was great news. Bruce had obviously managed to persuade Saros to let Stevie work in the kitchen.

One of his jobs was to fill the huge rain barrels with vinegar. Water could get rancid, and he had to put vinegar in the water to keep it fresh. Pure water was very precious on board the ship. Nobody was allowed to use fresh water to bathe in. They had to use the sea water. This was not very pleasant as you never felt truly clean. Even worse, salt would sometimes get in your eyes.

Once in the kitchen Stevie asked about the amazing spread he had laid.

Bruce, pretending to be hurt, grinned and said, "I have my secret weapon, look".

Pointing across to the stove Stevie saw a large white cormorant. It sat on a stool with its long legs crossed, wearing a pale blue cable knit jumper with matching beret. On the jumper was an embroidered initial 'F'.

"This is Fergal," said Bruce. "He is my Assistant Chef. I found him hiding in the back of the pantry. A stowaway. Fergal was cook on board *The Great White Shark*. The other cooks were jealous of him. They ganged up on him, and sabotaged a lot of his meals out of spite. The Captain of the ship threw him off ship. He is a fantastic cook as you will have seen from last night's meal. Luckily, he is a great swimmer and managed to swim to our ship as it was passing by."

Bruce finished rabbiting on and Fergal, getting off the stool, gave Stevie a bow. Bruce then told Fergal Stevie's name and the bird grabbed Stevie's hand, wrapping his hand feathers round his fingers in a friendly shake.

Stevie spoke saying, "The pirates are picking up more cargo at the next Island. It could be slaves. I think we should escape before we get to this Island. I heard one of the pirates mention the Feast of Molina. Witches and Warlocks will be going to Glendowwer for it. We could be part of the feast. I think my parents are at Glendowwer. I need to go there, but I need to get help as I cannot do it on my own."

Bruce in answer to Stevie said. "How can we escape? The deck is always full with crew at all times and you never know when you are being watched".

The three stood silently racking their brains until Stevie said "Is there any herbs you could place in their food to send them to sleep?"

"We don't have anything that strong" replied Bruce.

It was Fergal who suddenly came up with the answer. He flapped his wings excitedly. "I've got it –I've got it - there is a spell book in Ethan's room. Must have been Captains Cassons. I saw it when I took Ethan's supper in the bookcase the other night. It's bound to have something in there. I could take it when I drop his drink and sandwich off. I just need to get the timing right when Ethan's not in the cabin. If I stick it up my jumper nobody will see it".

"You would have to be very careful" said Stevie. "Ethan is no fool. Would it not be easier to rip a page out the book rather than take the book"?

"No" said Fergal. "I won't have time to go through it. I noticed when I dropped his tray off he went off to check the ship before he ate. But he was back by 9.15 pm. I just have to be quick before he comes back".

"It's very risky. You could get caught" said Bruce worried.

"Don't you think I take greater risks with you" said Fergal trying to make light of the matter.

"What do you mean"?

"Well if you got tipsy on ale you might try and have me as a snack".

The cormorant laughed at this but Bruce looked hurt.

"I would have to be pretty desperate to eat you. There's no meat on you. Where is food value on those twig legs"?

Looking at Fergal's long matchstick legs, and scrawny body he had a point. They all laughed.

"What type of name is Fergal for a Cormorant"?

"Hey you should talk. Stevie Rump. That's a bum joke".

"Old joke Fergal" said Stevie pretending to yawn, "Heard it all before. You are wasting your time with that one."

"Oh alright I'll stop teasing you with that one said Fergal. "Well it's agreed as far as I can see. I am going to see if I can get the book tonight so wish me luck."

The day passed quickly. When 9.15 pm came Fergal took a cup of tea, and supper to Ethan. He laid the tray carefully down on the wooden bedside table. Ethan was not in the room so must have left earlier for his walk on deck. This was a worry for Fergal as he didn't know how much time he had left.

The cabin was the largest room on board ship, with oak panelled doors. On the walls of the cabin hung pictures of pompous looking admirals. The bed was a single bed with white sheets, and a hair blanket. A compass, and telescope lay on the table, along with a black bear match holder. Looking across at the book shelf. It was filled with rows of mismatched sized books. The book Fergal had been looking for was not in its usual place.

Where was it?

He checked the shelf but it wasn't there. Fergal started to sweat heavily. Ethan could come back any time. He climbed up the bookshelves. Nothing there. He looked on the floor. There was clothes lying on there. Lifting them up him found the heavily embossed leather book.

On the front of the book was a picture of a large octopus being held by a witch upside down? Opening the book a large black slug fell out. He picked it up with his beak but dropped it on the ground. Better not eat it. It might do something strange to him he thought. Fergal then stuffed the book under his jumper. But it was bulky, and showed under his jumper. It was no good. He would have to rip some pages out.

All the while he listened for footsteps at the door in case Ethan caught him. Scanning the pages the book was titled "Elwyns Book of Magic. Something he had not noticed before. He flicked through the pages. Mermaid soup, cane toad breath, broomstick rash. Finally, he found something, a sleeping draught but would it work on Dog Pirates? This was for humans. He would take this page. He flattened it out and placed it under his jumper. The jumper lay smooth now so the outline of the paper could not be seen.

Placing the book back under the clothes on the floor. He was just in time. Ethan walked in.

Glancing at him briefly as Fergal walked out the door Ethan said "You have finished late".

Fergal stuttered "Sorry". His heart beating to a dozen.

"Next time you come in pick my clothes off the floor. Look how untidy you have left my room".

"Yes Sir. I will remember to do it next time".

"Make sure you do". Ethan's cold eyes looked through Fergal plainly irritated by him and turned his back on him.

Fergal walked to the door only breathing a sigh of relief. Once in the kitchen Fergal placed the page on the kitchen table. Reading the first line Stevie read out:

Take 1 kingfish eye and crush it blind
One feather of a sea bird pickkede from its rump
One spoon of brandye boil it well
Blood from a human boy
1 sharks tooth
1 cup of sage

1 lemon

1 wooden spike

1 large cobweb

1 rat's foot

Fergal then took over from Stevie reading the rest of the spell. Stevie came up from behind him, plucking a feather out of his skinny rump. Fergal screamed, and shot in the air, holding his backside. Then flew round the room dropping feathers everywhere. Full of rage he pecked at Stevie angrily.

Some of the feathers landed in the Kingfish soup Bruce had been making. Bruce annoyed fished them out.

"Get off "shouted Stevie, wincing and trying to ward off the angry bird. "Ouch stop it Fergal. We needed a feather for the spell" he shouted. But Fergal was not having any of it, and pecked Stevie on the shoulder, and would have pecked him more if the door hadn't opened.

It was Saros the Rottweiler.

"What's going on here?" snarled Saros. The three stopped everything they were doing. Horrified. The spell paper was on the floor. Saros stared at the mess in the kitchen.

"There was a rat in the kitchen. We tried to catch it. But it took off" piped up Bruce.

"Clean up this mess you idiots or I will have you thrown to the sharks – do you understand. Fetch me a drink" said Saros looking at Bruce.

While he was speaking to Bruce. Fergal quietly placed his large foot over the spell paper. Then started picking up the rest of his feathers scattered of the floor. Bruce quickly poured him a draught of ale.

Taking it from Bruce, Saros went to make his way out of the kitchen, but turned round giving the three a brief look. Then he muttered under his breath.

As the door shut Stevie said "Phew that was close. Come on let's get the rest of the spell done. It was a good job Fergal you sat on the spell paper".

Bruce read out the rest of the spell. "It says here blood from a human boy".

Stevie said "I need a pin"?

Bruce found a pin he used for whelks, washed it, and gave it to him. Stevie quickly pricked his finger. Blood came quickly. He held his finger over the basin as blood dripped into it. Then cleaned his finger with some stale vinegar water which made his finger sting.

Bruce dropped a lemon, and sage into the basin, along with brandy. A cobweb was found by the pantry door and placed in, as was a wooden spike. Bruce scooped up the wobbling eyeball out of its bloodied socket out of a kingfish. He was used to doing this but Stevie had to look away feeling quite sick.

With Bruce and Stevie preoccupied with the spell Fergal prepared the evening meal just in case anyone came in.

Bruce could not see any shark's teeth.

"Fergal do me a favour and see if there are any small sharks in the nets. If anyone asks just says it's for this evening meal. We can easily stick shark on tonight's menu. That's if the spell doesn't work".

As Fergal went on deck Bruce ground up the ingredients they had.

"Oh this is yuk" said Stevie "We need a rat's foot".

"I've got one. Go in in my brown satchel. It's hanging on the chair" said Bruce. "It's my toothbrush".

Stevie opened the satchel, and pulled out the dried out grey monstrosity, and handed it to him. The gruesome object went into the basin, just as Fergal came in with the small sharks.

"We're spoilt for choice "he shouted holding them by the fins. Then laid them on the kitchen table.

He picked up the largest of the sharks and prised a tooth out of its fishy mouth with his beak. But the tooth was sharp, and he cut his beak, blood, and sea water oozed on to the table. The tooth was then dropped into the basin. The ingredients were now all mixed up. Then all three of them chanted the final words to the spell.

Wictharrferannyff

Marwellwithsrarwin repeating this twice

Followed by a final chant of *Acranbarwynarrff.*

Nothing happened. They also had to cover their hands in the mixture while chanting these words. Apparently, covering their hands in the mixture would protect them from the spell.

Then out of the mixture came a silver, and blue fly. It flew up to the ceiling forming a figure of eight over Stevie, Bruce and Fergal's heads. Bruce had to resist the urge to swat it as it flew round him.

It continued making this figure of eight. Its silver wings making a mild drumming noise, which got louder and louder. Stevie became worried if it got any louder one of the Dog Pirates might come into the kitchen.

The other problem was that the ship would be due to arrive at Jack Island in an hour from what he had heard. Would the spell work in time? The noise then ceased.

Stevie, Fergal and Bruce found themselves pushed by some invisible force up to the ceiling. They could not get down and could only look at each other helplessly. They were then released, and fell to the ground with a resounding thud. Nursing their bruised arms, and legs they then brushed themselves down.

"What was all that about?" said Bruce wide eyed. The two others just shrugged. The mixture in the basin had overturned. It had now turned into an inky black liquid.

Checking everyone was not badly hurt Stevie grabbed a spoon, and scooped the liquid back into the basin. It made an odd hissing sound, as he poured it, careful to make sure it did not go on his hands. It seemed to be very hot now.

"I just hope the spell worked ". He said then went out of the kitchen, and peered outside. No-one appeared to have heard the commotion.

"Good" he said to himself. But it was strange. Normally, you would hear some activity. He shouted to the others to come outside and see if they could hear anything.

"Can you hear anything"? He asked again. But no there was not a sound. Not even the usual cussing from the sailors. All three went further on deck. The crew were lying where they fell. Some in distorted positions. Others lying across each other. All around the deck was total silence.

"It's like being in a dream" said Fergal. "This is so weird" he whispered to himself.

Nobody stirred as they went by. Fergal prodded Saros who lay on his back with his mouth wide open. He didn't look so frightening now. The beagle was lying beside him. A large piece of buttered bread wedged in his mouth. His eyes were open, but he was fast asleep. His silky coat was full of crumbs, and melted butter slipped down on to it.

None of them knew how long the spell would last so they decided to act quickly. They went back into the kitchen and reread the spell.

"The spell lasts one moon. That must be one night. Right let's get the boat out". As Stevie said this Bruce rounded up food from the kitchen. Placing it in a large wicker basket he threw in numerous loaves, wrapped salted pork, dried biscuits, and sardines, bottles of water, a fishing rod, compass, and map.

Fergal and Stevie untied the small fishing boat. Bruce then sat in it. Stevie then placed the oars in inside it. They then threw sackcloth in. Even though Bruce was plump, he was still the lightest being much shorter than the other two. He clutched the oars tightly. The basket of food he stuck between his legs to keep it steady.

Ropes were attached firmly to the boat as it was lowered into the sea. The two struggled with the rope as they lowered it as it kept slipping through their fingers. It might have been easier if there had been some grease on the rope but the sun had made it dry. The boat slowly lurched further towards the water. A basking sea turtle seeing the boat sped off furiously in the opposite direction.

Bruce hung on to the oars with his paws. Stevie had not even grabbed his case. Just a photo of his parents which was rolled up in his left trouser pocket. He hoped it didn't get wet.

Fergal wasn't bothered about possessions so as long as he had his beret, and jumper in the boat. Bruce had kept something precious. The last letter from his Auntie Lucy. She had bribed a magpie to give it to Bruce before the witches took her away. Bruce had placed it in a compartment in his collar. He could be a dark horse.

They were ready to go now. The boat lowered was bobbing on the surface of the sea.

Fergal climbed halfway down the rope, then half flew into the boat. The movement was effortless, being agile, and an excellent swimmer.

Not so for Stevie who awkwardly lowered himself further down the ship. He tried to not look at the huge waves crashing round the boat.

"Just look at the boat" he kept saying to himself. It willed him on. One wrong movement and he would be in the drink. Not being a strong swimmer he knew he would most certainly drown. He lowered himself further, and further down. At last nearly there, but just missed slipping, he fell clumsily into the boat, soaking the others with sea water.

They dried themselves with the sackcloth. The sackcloth would come in use later in the evening when the temperature dropped and it became cold.

Fergal then cut the ropes with his sharp beak. Stevie grabbed the oars. He would take the first turn at rowing. He worked fast with the oars because when darkness fell it would be difficult to see. They also did not know when the Dog Pirates would wake up, so the faster they worked it was less likely they would be captured.

Fergal had planned the route. They were going north to the Crimson caves. This was the exact opposite route to Glendowwer. A huge colony of monk seals lived there and could take them to the mermaids living there. Hopefully the mermaids would help them.

The mermaids were a strong race. The Queen of the Mermaids was Selena, but a spell had been placed on her by the Sea Witches so she could never enter the Caribbean Sea. It was not known where she was. Some people said the witches had killed her.

Stevie, Fergal and Bruce hoped they would get a sympathetic ear from the mermaids. Possibly get a group together who would go to Glendowwer, and rescue slaves being held there. But would they take note of a boy, a cat and a cormorant?

The waves were now getting wild, and crashed against the boat. Stevie's face covered in sweat. It dripped on to the oars making them slippery. It would take a couple of hours to get to Crimson Cave.

Stevie would have to do a full hours rowing. Fergal would then take over, then Bruce for a short while. An hour into the sail, Bruce had retrieved some bread, and salted pork from the basket they ate as they rowed. The three took it in turns to sip the bottle of water. Bruce was really suffering with the heat. His fur was soaking wet in clumps. His tongue lolled to one side. It would have been picture book with the brilliant sky line, and turquoise water if it had not been for the fact they were rowing with all their might so that "Black Scorpion" did not catch up with them.

A couple of routes the Dog Pirates would guess they had taken if they woke early Stevie hoped the pirates chose the wrong one.

Stevie had taken his top but this made him burn so he placed it back on. The top stuck to him in wet patches of sweat like glue...

Above them flew a circle of crows who now and again swooped down. The crows were waiting hungrily to see if the three would keel over with exhaustion. At one point a crow became quite brave and swooped down and pecked Fergal when it was his turn rowing.

Fergal full of rage attempted to swat it with an oar, but the boat nearly capsized.

Stevie grabbed the oar. Glaring at a shamefaced Fergal. He took it back, and continued rowing ignoring the smirking crows. However, when it began to get dark the crows flew off losing interest in the three.

With darkness falling Bruce's night sight would come be handy. They had rationed the food. But vinegar water had made their mouths dry.

Finally in the distance Bruce could make something out that looked like a pink speck. "I can see something".

Stevie, who had nearly fallen asleep grabbed the telescope.

"This could be the Crimson Caves" Stevie shouted. "I think it is – it must be. We have followed the map. It is the first Island we should be seeing after all this time". The three could have wept with relief.

Bruce continued rowing for twenty minutes. Stevie then took over. They finally reached the moonlit beach. Worn out with the heat. They dragged the boat right up to the beach.

Standing up shakily on the white powdered sand. Their feet sank into clumps of sea weed. But it was heaven on their hot feet. They rubbed their faces, and bodies with cool sea water. Then dragged the boat further up. Pink dusky coloured caves faced them. There was three caves to choose from. They chose the third cave.

Once in the cave with the boat near them, they glanced round. It was empty. They took their belongings out of the boat and covered it with drift wood, and tree branches.

In the cave all Bruce could think about was food. He rubbed sticks together, made a fire then fried soggy sardines he had brought with him. The three had it with chunks of bread.

What they thought was a small cave, turned out to be a huge cave leading off to three tunnels. They were tired so thought they would explore tomorrow. The sandy cave was hard to lie on so they used bits of tree branches to make up beds. Bruce then took the sack cloth out of the boat, and cut it into three strips so they could use them as a bed cover for each of them.

The fire was now nearly going out but it still gave the cave some warmth. They then part covered the entrance of the cave with tree branches. When the fire had nearly extinguished, the three were now fast asleep. As they slept hundreds of spiders watched over them. Even Bruce's loud snoring didn't wake the others up. They slept on for five hours.

Bruce woke up first and could make out a black line moving. Rubbing his eye and sitting up he looked closer.

What he saw was an army of spiders going to the direction of one of the tunnels.

"Look at that "he said to the others who were now waking up. "Shall we follow them"?

"I'm not sure "said Fergal "What if there is a giant spider ready to eat us the end of the tunnel – have you seen the size of some of those spiders".

Stevie said "Well we've got to move on, and we only have a few choices of directions to go – let's follow them"?

Bruce agreed but Fergal was still suspicious, and followed behind the pair reluctantly as they made their way through the tunnel.

The spiders were fast walkers, and the three had to speed up. The cave had sharp corners, as they followed. It was like going round a giant wheel. The sharp corners scraped a part of Fergal's feathers as he went round .His feathers were sore and felt burnt. He cussed aloud but the noise of it reverberated round the tunnel.

"Be quiet" said Stevie "You will cause rocks to fall on us."

Fergal glared at him but kept quiet anyway.

As they came round the final corner. They came to a giant turquoise rock pool Peering into the crystal clear water they saw a most peculiar sight, the spiders were climbing into the rock pool in droves, swimming deeper, and deeper into it. They now looked like tiny tad poles.

Bruce dipped his paw into the water causing a ripple, the spiders swam further into the water. Along the top of the water appeared a large golden fish. Bruce excitedly put his paw further along the water straining to reach it. He then put both paws in, as he couldn't quite grasp it. Stretching forward he brushed it with his paw "I think I've nearly got it" he shouted to the others.

Fergal and Stevie tried to grab Bruce legs as he now was hanging over the rock pool, but his legs slipped through their grasp. He fell deep into the rock pool.

Chapter Six

Terrified, Bruce tried to cling to the corner of the rock pool, but he fell deeper and deeper into it, falling through deep caverns. He kept falling. The water appeared not to touch him now.

He heard a faint shout from the other, but he still kept on falling. Their voices appeared now to be a long distant echo. He did not appear to need air, and could breathe. He thought he would most certainly drown. All his weight appeared to be lifted from him. His body felt light. Starting to feel at ease, he tried to swipe at the shoals of little silver fish that floated by. He kept missing. The fish appeared to glide through his paws. Losing interest he looked further down into the caverns.

As he travelled more marine appeared before him. Large turtles swam past him. Even tiny pink sea horses, who, appeared to be going in and out miniature coral houses. There now appeared to be an activity with shoals of multi coloured fish looking at him as they swam past. Finally, he fell with a thud to the bottom of the sea bed.

Mermaid children swam past him, carrying satchels bulging with books. Their silver, and purple tails glistening fell into zig zag ripples as they swam by. The mer children were very fair, with pointed ears and thin faces. Their eyes appeared to be either blue, or green. Most of them had fair hair. Some of them had red hair. The older mermaids had hair which was like a coarse rope, and hung in huge plaits down their backs. They did not seem to be surprised to see him.

"Where am I?" he asked a lone mer boy swimming.

The boy turned round looking surprised "Why it's Pink Bay of course". He looked at Bruce as if he was mad

"Sorry" said Bruce "I'm a stranger round here and arrived here accidentally you could say".

He added "I am lost I'm trying to find my way back to my friends".

The mer boy became friendly "Hi my name is Liam I would love to able to show you round here but I have to get to school. I have had two school late tickets. If I get one more. I get detention for a month. I live with my parents at Blue Bay- it's easy to find your way round everything is in colours. This is pink bay, further down is Lilac Bay, when you get past Lilac Bay you will come to Blue Bay where I live. If you see a number 20 it's my parent's house. I am sure they will help you". He started swishing his tail "Good luck have to go Mrs Gershwin gets really annoyed if you are late". He swam off so fast Bruce didn't even have time to thank him.

Bruce still could not believe. He had not drowned the water. It just felt like a slightly warm air. Breathing was not a problem. Walking on the sea bed floor felt light. But now he was feeling very alone. His friends would think he was dead.

Brushing tears away from his whiskers, desperately wanting to get back to them. But how could he when he was completely lost. It was hard not to imagine what his friends would be thinking. They probably thought he had drowned. This was no good feeling sorry for himself. It would be no help to him.

A large fish which to his horror appeared to be some type of shark brushed past him causing a huge ripple. He was lucky it seemed to be preoccupied and didn't seem to be the slightest bit interested in him.

Swimming along he noticed the mer boy had been right. All houses were all in colours. They all were like large giant beach huts with wooden verandas. They even had small front gardens filled with what looked like hollyhocks and sweet peas. How bizarre.

There was a house larger than the others it was café called "Stingray Café". The door of the café was heavy. It was like walking into a safe. The ceiling was low. Bruce felt his collar.

His savings were in a secret compartment but would they take his money? Feeling hungry. There was lovely smells coming from the kitchen he picked up a menu.

A large octopus dressed in a starched white apron came to take his order. Before he even looked at the order he showed his money to her and said "Do you take this money?

She looked at it and said "You an Islander?

He nodded and she smiled and said "No problem".

He looked happily at the menu consisting of red snapper omelette, kingfisher bites with onion rings, Coral iced cake, mud pie, apple cake, sand cake, oyster ice cream with chocolate biscuits. The list was endless. He had never had food like this. The menu even had illustrations of the food.

Taking a long time choosing and thinking "I wonder what fries are? He ordered sea sausages, with fries, and beans then a large surprise chocolate cake with ice cream. Purring to himself he thought best he should find his way back to the other on a full stomach.

The waitress had curly blonde hair, and a huge gaping mouth covered in red lipstick. She had a cockney accent, and as she took the order she nibbled away at a dog eared pencil. Placing this behind her ear she walked to the counter and placed his order with the chef.

There was other people in the café. A group of blue crabs were laughing, and joking in a corner. They were dressed in tiny blue overalls. They had ordered the vegetable soup, but one orange coloured crab did not appear to be able to hold the bowl properly, constantly spilling the soup. The larger of the crabs started teasing him about it. Then others joined in laughing at him. The orange crab shook a large claw at them, but they still continued laughing at him.

Furious he grabbed the main tormenter by the collar of his overall, the table nearly overturned, with the soup spilling over the tablecloth.

The waitress seeing her white starched tablecloth getting stained, marched over. Grabbing the larger of the crabs by the shoulder she shouted "Pack it in or I will throw you out".

Meekly the large crab looked at the rim of the tablecloth, and whispered "sorry" meekly.

The waitress then marched off. Her high heels clicking on the finely polished floor. She could handle herself, she rarely had any trouble in the café.

When Bruce's order arrived he was in heaven. The sea sausages dark brown, sizzled, and were enormous with fries spilling over the plate. He covered them in ketchup, taking a bite he closed his eyes enjoying every mouthful. Tasting the fries, he now knew what fast food was.

Soon his plate was cleared and he opened the compartment in his collar, and looked at the coins the waitress had given him as change.

The two coins had a picture of Selena the Mermaid carved on it. They were silver rimmed in pink, and weighed the same as ordinary coins.

When his pudding arrived he could hardly eat it. Chocolate covered his whiskers as he bit into the oozing cake. The frosted chocolate buttons topping started buzzing, and fruit jellies exploded in his mouth. The little cat purred with delight.

Stevie and Fergal would love this café he thought. But he would have to get a move on, and find an opening back into the rock pool. Giving a final stretch he got out of his chair, and waved good bye to the waitress, who nodded, and continued polishing trays of cutlery. As he came out of the cafe, he made his way past the lilac houses, coming to blue bay as Liam had mentioned. It was here the houses turned into tiny hamlets.

The houses were now circular shaped with small square chimneys. One had a black and white mer cat playing by itself outside. It sniffed at Bruce, but made no attempt to speak to him.

Puzzled he said "Hello" but it looked blankly at him.

Maybe the cats round here can's speak he thought to himself. As the cat strode off Bruce became aware it had a little fish tail. A tiny silver tail and even gills. It was as if the little cat had half turned into a fish.

"Crikey" thought Bruce" I hope that doesn't happen to me".

Bruce worried caught his reflection in a strange contraption with wheels parked outside a house. He could see his face it. His fur gleamed, his normal tabby fur was now a brilliant auburn colour. His white paws were no longer a dingy white, even his fleas felt like they had gone. Touching his feet he checked to make sure they hadn't turned into a fish tail. They hadn't.

Swimming along further he saw a shrimp on a bicycle delivering plankton to various houses, seeing Bruce it did a wheelie in front of him. Grinning cheekily, it did another one as it passed him.

What an incredible place thought Bruce. Everything had an air of eccentricity about it. It would have been a great place to live if he had the others with him.

The next person he saw was a mermaid sweeping sand with a broom from her front garden. He would ask her if there was a way out. Someone must know.

The others meanwhile were still in a state of shock. They truly believed Bruce had drowned. They had stretched as far as they could over the rock pool to try and catch him. Fergal holding Stevie's legs to see if he could see anything. It was all been in vain.

"I wonder if there is another way round the rock pool we might see Bruce has been swept out to sea" said Stevie. There was an air of gloom. They both did not really want to say what they really thinking.

Stevie tearful said "Come on let's go through the cave and see if there is an underwater stream. He might have ended up along that. "

Some of the spiders were still in the cave and appeared to be following Fergal and Stevie.

"What do they want?" said Fergal. "They can't speak so why are they following us"? He repeated the questions again to the spider's this time exasperated.

The next minute more spiders gathered forming in large black clumps. It was like watching a dance formation. Some were in straight lines, some were in curved.

Stevie and Fergal watched in wonderment. Words starting to form with their bodies on the cave floor.

"Follow us" the words the spiders had created said.

They then formed another group it said "We can help you".

Stevie and Fergal looked at each other "What have we got to lose" said Stevie to Fergal.

"Let's follow them but no stretching over rock pools" said Fergal.

They then followed behind the spiders. The spiders marched further, and further into another cave. The ground smelt musty. There was a smell of damp about it. There seemed to be a bright light coming in but they couldn't see where it was coming came from.

The floor started getting more slippery, and Stevie had to go very slowly, having to hold on to stones when he thought he was going to fall, and only just managed to stop himself going over a couple of times.

Fergal sneezed a couple of times which made an echo round the cave. The spiders finally came to another rock pool and crawled up to it.

"They did this before "said Fergal suspiciously "and look what happened. We lost Bruce".

Stevie ignoring this and walked up to the rock pool, and peered in. Fergal followed but stood back. They peered into the water of the rock pool it cleared they could see their reflections very clearly.

Stevie was now very tanned. His hair very fair. He even seemed taller.

Fergal was very pleased with his. The reflection did not appear to show his scars on his beak. Fergal smiled back at the handsome bird that looked back at him. His white feathered body a sharp contract to Stevie's.

"Hello Stephen" a voice said breaking out of nowhere. Stevie and Fergal startled jumped. They looked around but couldn't see anyone.

The voice spoke again "Do not be afraid I will not harm you". Stevie peered back into the rock pool which was now clearing and turned into a pastel pink. The water then became bubbly.

To his amazement a face appeared. The face was that of an old lady. Haggard, with a long grey hair, and blue eyes. Once again she started to speak.

I am Selena, Queen of the Mermaids of the blue, and lilac seas. Gledwyn imprisoned me in this rock pool. I need you to free me – please help me. Humans are the only ones that can free me".

"How do we know you how can we trust you? Bruce has disappeared we want to find what happened to him. He was fine until he appeared into a rock pool similar to the one you are in" replied Stevie getting over his fear.

"My people" she spoke sadly "are in grave danger. They need me to help them. Gledwyn aims to take over the whole of the sea, and make them her slaves. She is gathering up forces. Lives will be lost. The oceans will be destroyed".

"Can you help us find out what has happened to Bruce?" said Stevie.

"I can "she said "I also know everything about you, I know Stephen that your family were captured by Sea Witches and they are at Glendowwer.

She added "Help me and I will help you that I promise you".

"How do we know you are not Gledwyn?" said Fergal finally speaking.

"Do you not think if I was Gledwyn I would have captured you by now, and not wasted time talking to you" said Selena.

"What do you know of my parents"? Stevie asked almost bursting with excitement when he realised what she had said.

"They are safe" said Selena "But they are prisoners in the tower at Glendowwer".

"What about Bruce"?

"Ahh Bruce the little cat. You do not have to worry. He is safe, and enjoying his food. My friends will keep him safe. See for yourself look into the rock pool" Selena replied with a slight smile.

Her face disappeared. Looking in the rock pool they saw Bruce. He appeared to be gliding along as if on skis. He then stopped to talk to a mermaid. Fergal and Stevie beamed at the little figure but he could not see them. They shouted his name but he could not hear them. They looked at each other relieved he was safe.

The water in the rock pool then rippled, and Selena's face returned.

"Why did he not drown in the water?" asked Fergal puzzled.

"The water as you go deeper turns into an air so you can breathe easily" said Selena in reply. "However, if a human fell into the water they would drown."

She then added "If Bruce remains in the water another 24 hours he will develop a tail, and gills. He will also lose the power of speech. It is urgent you get him out as soon as possible".

The thought of Bruce as a type of mermaid made Fergal laugh guiltily. "He would eat his tail" he said. Can you imagine that he loves fish ".

Stevie didn't reply he was thinking about if they didn't get to Bruce in time.

"Can you show me my parents?" asked Stevie to Selena.

"I can" she replied and her reflection disappeared once again.

Out of the swirling rock pool Stevie saw his parents sitting in a dark room. They looked very sad, and were with a lot of children all clustered together. He recognised the children. They were his school friends. There was also a lot of other children he didn't recognise... Seeing them made him cry. He felt their anguish. Tears dripped off his face.

Fergal stroked his arm helplessly. "At least they are safe" said Fergal gently.

The reflection of Stevie's parents disappeared, and Selena's face came back. Stevie and Fergal looked at each other.

"It makes sense to help her. After all we came here to get help from the mermaids remember" said Stevie to Fergal. Who was still suspicious but after seeing Bruce he felt they did not have a lot of choice if they wanted to see him again.

"I need you to be brave" said Selena breaking into their conversation "What I asking you to do is not an easy thing to do". She added. "The spiders are my friends they will help you. They have been feeding me or I would have surely perished.

To set me free you need to enter The Black Cave, jump into the rock pool. You will be quite safe, and be able to breathe, and swim the way Bruce does. I will Stephen give you an amulet to wear so you can breathe. You, Fergal will be able to breathe perfectly. My friends the spiders will show you the amulet Stephen you are to wear. There is a pouch place it round your neck you will need to place the emerald key in it. The emerald key will be near on an oyster bed. It will not be far from where you fall. Once the key is in the pouch, it will remain safe. Once you are on the ocean sea bed you will be not far from Horobin the Hermits Cave. I will send word to him that you are coming you will need to say the words "Matuszuska".

He will then greet you as a friend. It is the word I and my friends use .They are the only ones who know this word. He will then take you to the Oyster Cave which is half a mile away. You will find the Emerald Oyster there".

She was silent for a moment but then spoke again saying "You will also encounter Roat the Reef Shark. You must hide from him. He will be too busy eating all the shoals of fish. You should be safe".

"A Reef Shark "said Fergal horrified "You have to be kidding. We have to be careful so it doesn't have us as a little meal"!!!

Selena replied "My friends will try and protect you".

Stevie tweaked his friend's beak to gain his attention. This made Fergal more annoyed.

"Look" Stevie said "We have to do this but just be careful. Let's do it Fergal for Bruce and my parent's sake".

Selena spoke again. "Bruce does not have much time before he develops a tail. He will then have to remain underwater for ever".

Chapter Seven

Fergal and Stevie, saddened at the thought of Bruce remaining underwater forever, nodded in agreement to each other.

"We don't have any choice then Selena please get the spiders to lead us to the rock pool. We will help you "said Stevie.

The second he spoke he heard a large drumming noise. The spiders were forming a platoon of soldiers. They had piled up high on each other.

Moving to a large rock in the cave, Stevie and Fergal helped them move it, being careful not to crush any of the tiny spiders with their feet.

Underneath was a black leather pouch inside a silver amulet wrapped in black string. Stevie placed the pouch round his neck. The black string acting as a necklace.

Selena's voice suddenly reverberated round the cave. "Follow the spiders".

"How do we get back "?

"Go back to the place where you first fell in the sea. It will be by a huge horse shoe shaped rock. The spiders will guide you"

The spiders appeared in a line in front of them and Stevie and Fergal then followed the spiders. They were as usual racing ahead in a long formation. Fergal tripped a couple of times, trying to keep up with them. Stevie didn't have that problem. Fergal thought that it must be because Stevie's huge banana feet helped him move better. The spiders had now arrived at the rock pool. It was at the far end of the cave. The cave was more prehistoric than the rest of the cave. It had huge sharp, black, jagged edged spikes sticking out the walls, even the ground had something resembling coal dust on it. Sparkling as they walked on it.

As they walked clumsy, short sighted bats flew over their heads until they finally reached the rock pool.

The spiders stopped at the edge of another rock pool. Stevie stripped off to his underclothes. One at a time they climbed nervously into the water.

They sank deeper, and deeper, into the whirling rock pool. It was like falling into a large well. Suddenly their bodies were spinning. They fell further down into the water. The spinning went on, and on, then with a loud thud they both fell to the bottom of the rock pool.

The water was getting duller, and duller finally turning into a dismal grey. There was no strong colours at the bottom of the rock pool. It looked very bleak.

The horse shoe rock Selena had mentioned was on the bottom of the sea where they fell .It was a large rock so would be easy to see when they came back thought Stevie if they were successful in finding the emerald key. But what would happen if they were not successful?

He tried to put this thought out of his mind. He did not have time to worry about that at the moment.

Shoals of white fish swam by them. Fergal and Stevie walked on the bottom of the rock pool. The sea water was now a milky blue so visibility was easier.

They could now see rows of what looked like little beach houses and passed a pointy turreted house, they swam by two sea horses, and a turtle.

Swimming further along coming to a most peculiar house. It was yellow with a pink thatched roof and very narrow yellow window sills. It looked like a Battenberg cake, even the shutters were a pale pink. The roof puffed out billowing white puffs of smoke. Walking up the sea weed path the sign post said "Horobins".

"Look "said Stevie "It's the house of Horobin just as Selena said". Fergal answering was once again suspicious "Seemed too easy to find". Leading up to the door were tiny sign posts "Do not stand on the seaweed". Do not loiter" "Do not walk on my garden" If you are selling anything clear off". The final sign said "I do not need any windows or doors so go away".

Fergal and Stevie finally reached the front door. Stevie knocked on the bulldog faced door knocker. The whole house seemed to shake as he rapped on the knocker. There was a spy hole on the knocker.

An eye peered out saying in a mild Scottish accent "Who is it"?

Stevie and Fergal looked at each "Matuszuska"" they both said in unison.

"We are friends of Selena" said Stevie.

The door opened slightly and the voice said "I help no-one go away- why do I never get any peace?"

"Selena is in trouble she said you would help her" said Stevie.

"Why should I care about her if she is in trouble "said the voice exasperated?

Stevie said "Look we don't have much time we are trying to help Selena and our friend. If you are a friend of the mermaids you will help us please "

The door opened wider. Finally Stevie and Fergal came face to face with the owner of the voice. Facing them was a little black prawn dressed in green overalls. Horobin eyed the pair up and down, and did not seem to be impressed with what he saw. He sniffed into a large white handkerchief.

"Selena is dead" he said

"No, she is not" said Stevie adding "She is imprisoned in a rock pool. We really need to get the emerald key to set her free. She told us to say the words "Matuszuska to you".

Horobin seemed shaken and said "Nobody knows that word apart from her. I hope I can trust you both. I am one of few who know this word. She helped me and my family and I owe her a great debt".

He turned his back on them and appeared to be thinking to himself "I will "he said "Show you the way to Oyster Cave but I will have to leave you there then you are own. The risk is too great" He sneezed into his wet handkerchief. His black eyes became watery. It was strange to see they were underwater but the water was like an air not making you wet.

"Thank you Horobin" said Stevie.

Horobin went back into his house, and came back out a few minutes later. He then locked his front door placing the key under one of his numerous sign posts.

They walked or glided for two miles passing an old ship wreck. Out of it appeared a pink octopus which grabbed at fish swallowing them up as they went by.

Fergal had been curious but then worried he would see skeletons looked away. Feeling shivers go down his spine. The further they walked the larger the fish had become. It was creepy. The air felt colder. They went past dark caves. They could hear loud noises, which Stevie thought might be whales. He hoped they were not sharks.

They finally arrived at Oyster Cave. It shone pearl white against the gloomy sea. Sparkling diamond, and silver lights came out of it.

"Well "said Horobin. "This is where I leave you- I'm off. I hope you make it – watch out for sharks" and waved good bye to the pair. He then scuttled off.

Stevie and Fergal looked at each other. The word sharks sent a chill down them. They had seen the horror they had inflicted on the seamen.

Once they reached the cave, the brightness disappeared. Inside the entrance of the cave hundreds of silver fish swam past them. Huge jelly like fish brushed against them, followed by sea snakes. As they swam they came across more ship wrecks.

Fergal caught sight of a skeleton hanging over the side of a ship. He quickly looked away quickly. A sea slug tried to get into his mouth, and he brushed it away disgustedly. His heart was beating so fast he really thought it would burst. The whole place was getting more and more eerie.

He looked at Stevie for reassurance, but he was not much better. Sea snakes were trying to wrap round his shoulders. Unfastening the sticky creatures they glided off.

They swam a quarter of a mile into the cave. Sea spiders had now joined sea snakes. They all appeared to be travelling in the same direction.

"How will we know where the emerald key is Stevie"?

Stevie shrugged in reply. It felt like they were looking for a needle in a haystack. Transparent spiders floated past them. Their bodies alone were size of a dinner plate.

Thank heavens they can't harm us thought Stevie.

There was worse to come. Shoals of sea slugs clung to them as they swam further into the cave. Stevie felt sick. The slime from their bodies clung to his arms. He managed to entangle himself from them. Fergal had pecked at one which had slimed on his beak much to his disgust. It tasted bitter and he spat it out.

Stevie and Fergal continued swimming further into the cave, which appeared to be lighter now. This was fine for visibility, but the down side was that you could see more sea monstrosities. Huge two headed red snakes swam past them, orange cat fish, and a fish with a rhino head, and damsel fish added to the strange underwater collection.

Coming deeper into the cave, they came into what looked like a deserted temple. There was a stone alter, and on the sea floor was hundreds of oyster beds.

"The key could be in one of these oysters "said Stevie adding ""But there are hundreds how on earth will we know which one to open?"

Fergal sighed in reply. He tried to open one of the oysters with a rock. It would not budge, and remained tightly shut. They tried opening a dozen others all without success. They remained shut.

"Look" said Fergal "What if I ask a passing fish if they know where the emerald key is"?

"No" said Stevie "It's too dangerous. They might be friends of the Sea Witches".

Fergal said "We have to ask someone. This is hopeless".

Stevie ignored him and swam off frantically searching the oyster bed for one oyster he hoped would stand out. Frustrated, he tried to concentrate on the rows upon rows of oysters. If they didn't get the key and get back quickly Bruce would be doomed to spend his life underwater. He had to keep searching.

The sound of bubbling water made him look across to where a noise was coming from. In the distance he could see a human shape. The vision became clearer. It was a young mermaid. But she appeared to be crying.

"Are you a ghost?" asked the little mermaid.

"No" said Stevie I am a boy and I am looking for an emerald key- have you heard of it"? He asked her.

She said "no" slightly backing away from him "I have never heard of it" she then rubbed at her tear stained eyes.

"I will not hurt you" said Stevie "My friend and I are looking for this key to help Selena the Mermaid".

The little mermaid appeared to relax when she heard this and said. "I have heard of her - but my mother said the witches have her".

Stevie replied "Yes they have imprisoned her. We are going to set her free that's why we need the key".

He looked round for Fergal. He was nowhere to be seen. Where was? Thinking he had gone off to look for the emerald key he continued in his search. The little mermaid followed him now not so nervous of him but curious.

"What is your name"?

"Tia "she replied.

"Why were you are you crying Tia"?

"I am due to play in the sea choir .I have lost my notes so I don't know my lines. Rosebud and Apple have theirs, and I'll look stupid". She burst into tears. Her tiny mermaid tail swishing around her as she cried.

Stevie put his arm round her and said "Don't worry you might be able to remember your lines. I find if I repeat things twice or thrice my memory comes back. Try singing the song. See what happens".

"But I don't know the song" she wiped the tears off her face.

"Yes you do" said Stevie. "Think hard and sing whatever comes into your head".

"Umm sapphires and gold and diamond rings "she sang. "No. that's not right". She started again. She faltered then started singing again. To her amazement the song came out of her mouth perfectly. She had one of the sweetest voices. She sang the song all the way through. Then continued singing it again.

Hearing a quaking noise Stevie turned to where the noise was coming from. To his amazement all the oyster shells had opened in unison while she sang. The minute she stopped the shells closed.

"Keep singing Tia "said Stevie.

She did as she was told. He quickly scanned the open oyster shells. Her singing created a grand opera... Crabs swimming by joined in. Even a passing seal opened its black whiskered mouth, and sang in soprano. It was truly magical. Stevie swam along the rows of oyster shells with their mouths open. When he had almost given up, a dark green glistening object appeared to be in one of the oyster shells.

It was an emerald key!

Excitedly he prised it from the shell. Just in time as Tia had abruptly stopped singing and the shell closed with a snap.

He then turned to Tia and shouted "Thank you".

Tia waved happily. She had now remembered all her lines and then swam away to her music class.

The emerald key he placed on a chain round his neck in the leather pouch. But where was Fergal? Stevie started to worry.

He would never have been gone this long why hadn't he come back? Where had he gone?

Chapter Eight

Meanwhile, Bruce had been having a whale of a time. He had made many friends. A lot of the mermaids had warned him about Gledwyn. He had heard horror stories about mer children being stolen, and sold into slavery by the witches.

Coming into the cosy hamlets the witches had swam underwater in droves, breaking doors down, grabbing children in front of their hysterical parents. Any brave parents trying to save their children were held back by Roat the Reef Shark, and Hammerhead sharks. It seemed nothing could be done about the witches since Selena had gone.

Bruce had been amazed at how well he was now swimming. No longer clumsy, turning into a very strong swimmer. He could ride huge waves now just like the mermaids, and sea horses. His fur was now completely waterproof. He was fitter, and healthier than he had ever been.

But he missed Stevie, and Fergal and was desperate to see them. The other thing was he was completely lost. The fish he had made friends had made him feel guilty. He had in his lifetime he thought eaten many of their relatives.

Now he was eating edible plants. Something completely unknown to him. The underwater sea weed tasted like liquorice eating even eaten red sea jelly which lay in clusters at the bottom of the sea. It tasted like the real thing but the Stingray Café was his God.

He still had money left but it wouldn't last forever. He knew he had to be more careful. There was a lot of labourer's maybe he could get work he thought in that field. But it was not something he wanted to do. All he wanted was to get out of the water and get back to the cave. No-one had heard of the cave he had continually asked mer folk about it.

He tried not to be negative about not getting out. That would be losing hope. Not something in his makeup.

Bruce managed to find an abandoned enormous oyster shell as a little home for himself, he had stuck a name on it "Bruce's". It had tiny windows. Inside it had an abandoned brown wool sofa and nothing else. That would do if he had to get away from predator fish he thought.

Still trying various routes to get back to the Crimson Caves but he always seemed to end up going in a circle. Also, a strange things happened every time he tried a different route something bit his ankles. It kept happening. The water had not been clear enough to see what was doing this. It was very annoying.

Carpentry was not his subject but he managed to make a small bed out of a wooden box. Being underwater was great but he did not want to be here for the rest of his life, later today he would try going up Tammy Lane. Maybe he would find a way out there. Having not gone far up this route as it was full of sea snakes, who, although were harmless got stuck in his fur.

Eating some sea jelly he asked a passing seal if he had heard of the Crimson Cove. As usual the answer was no. But he continued anyway. The sea became darker and colder. Sea slugs and snakes brushed passed him. It was no concern to him. They eyed him up with curiosity but then glided by.

His heart was in his mouth sometimes by the sheer size of some of the fish, and their huge teeth. They ignored him and went off in great shoals.

Suddenly, he saw a high silver fin. This was big trouble. Instinct told him what it was. A reef shark.

He swam to a huge rock, and squeezed behind it. The huge fish became clearer. It was at least ten feet long. Its large dark eyes looking at the terrified fish frantically swimming for their lives.

The water bubbled as the race to save themselves started. The shark looking bored grabbed a large orange fish, and swallowed it whole, then started on another, and then another one. The shark burped, then started on another one.

Bruce squeezed further down into the rock. It was getting a tight fit, and the sharp edges scratched his sides. He dared not breathe. The shark was getting nearer to him, eating more, and more fish. Something touched him. He dared not look round. It touched his back. He whimpered to himself, and kicked it with his foot.

"Stop it Bruce you idiot, it's me Stevie" came a whisper. "Fergal and I came to find you ".

Bruce was so excited he almost forgot about the shark and was about to come out of the rock. Stevie grabbed, and pushed him further down into the rock.

"Ow "said Bruce

"Quiet" said Stevie "The shark is getting nearer".

Stevie could hear Bruce's heart beating ten to a dozen. He held on to him. The shark had now got very close to them but now appeared to be vomiting up orange fish. It had had more than its fill and swam further up into the water. It then disappeared from sight. Bruce and Stevie stayed put for another ten minutes. There was silence now.

Bruce came out of the rock. His paws were scratched by the jagged rock but he didn't care, giving Stevie a hug. His legs wobbled from beneath him. He was now so excited to see his friend he began purring and could not stop. After ten minutes, the shark had not come back and it was then they relaxed.

Stevie then told Brue about Selena. Peeping out of crevices in the coral listening to the pair were hundreds of fish. They had hidden there when they the shark appeared...

"We have to look for Fergal "said Stevie.

"Do you think he's just got lost?" asked Bruce.

"I don't know it's as if he has disappeared into thin air".

They searched the dark caverns in the sea. Fergal was nowhere to be seen. Giant slugs hung from coral and stuck on them as they searched. Extricating themselves from the slime which left white trails on their body, they continued their search. Stevie was getting very worried. That shark had been very near them.

Bruce too was worried. Ecstatic at seeing Stevie but now thinking about Fergal had taken the edge off it.

Bruce asked passing mermaids if they had seen him. They hadn't.

Finally, they passed an older mermaid called Nadille and asked if she had seen Fergal. She was one of the oldest members of the mermaids. Nature had been cruel to her. She had a sanguine completion, a bent nose, full lips, and small green eyes. Most mermaid wore their hair in braids. She had cut her hair close to the scalp. Her skin was rubbery. When she spoke one of her teeth wobbled dangerously on her bottom jaw.

"Wasn't that the stupid bird"? A cormorant I think" said Nadille nastily. "I kept telling him to keep off the orange path. It's a haven for witches on the lookout for mer children". He said he had to find something sharp and wouldn't listen".

Stevie could not understand why Fergal had done this. Why would he swim so far away from Stevie? It did not make sense.

They went cautiously down the orange path but he was not there. Stevie decided they had to go back to Selena. She would help them.

Besides he had just accidentally trodden on Bruce's foot. Stevie had seen in horror that Bruce's feet were turning webbed. His tail was now thin, and shiny almost like leather. Bruce who was blind as a bat hadn't noticed this.

It was best he hadn't thought Stevie. He would be hysterical.

"Bruce" said Stevie "We will have to go back to Selena".

"What about Fergal"? Bruce asked.

"It will be quicker if Selena helps us" said Stevie.

It was a horrible thought leaving their friend behind, but they had no choice. Selena would help them. That Stevie was sure of as he touched the emerald key at his throat. It was still safe in the pouch. That was the main thing, and his only way to barter to help Fergal.

Stevie had memorised points as they swam along. They were getting nearer to Horobbin's cave and then would not far from where he and Fergal had originally landed.

The water was getting unnaturally darker, and felt much colder. The pair struggled to see ahead of them. A black shoal of lumbering shapes were above their heads. These were not sharks. Stevie caught sight of a dark bony foot nearly touching him. Grabbing hold of Bruce in the dark he dragged him further down into the sea.

"Sea Witches "he whispered "Get down". Bruce obeyed quickly.

The witches appeared to have brought a swarm of black flies with them which buzzed round the pair.

They waited until it was clear, and set off again, just relieved the witches hadn't seen them. The water began to get clearer.

"It must have been the witches causing the dark shadows" said Bruce. The water was so clear now you could all around you.

They were now at Horobbins house. But the house had been wrecked. All the sign posts ripped. They knocked on the door. There was no answer.

A turtle Stevie had seen before came up to Bruce and whispered "Sea Witches have taken him".

Horrified Stevie asked "Why".

"The Feast of Molina" the turtle replied sorrowfully. "He will be part of the meal along with a lot of my other friends".

The house had been daubed in black paint in black stripes on the walls. It was a very sorry sight.

The pair said "Goodbye" to the sad eyed turtle. Stevie feeling guilty Horobbin had helped him.

Bruce had never met Horobbin but he too felt for him. He was also thinking of Fergal. They walked further ending up at the horse shoe rock.

"What do we do now"? Bruce asked.

"We wait" said Stevie. They did not have to wait long hearing a rush of water. A mini water fall came pouring down. The waterfall did not touch them. Out of the waterfall appeared a rope ladder. It now lay straight in front of them

"Come on" said Stevie "I will go first. You follow me".

Stevie got on the first rung. The waterfall had subsided, and the water was now calm. It would be easy to climb up and the first couple of rungs... He went half way up with Bruce following him. The ladder wobbled, but they held on tight.

There seemed to be an orange orb guiding them at the top of the ladder. The ladder was long, both Stevie and Bruce's arms ached. They kept on. It seemed as if they were climbing the ladder forever. They both dared not look down.

By now Stevie had nearly reached the top. He could see the rock pool entrance. Sighting a black swarm on the surface, he realised it was the spiders. Sighing with relief he climbed the final rung, hanging on to the sides of the rock pool to get out. He was exhausted and sat on the cave floor.

Bruce appeared a short while later. Stevie helped him out. They were both pleased to be back on land, and out of the water.

The spiders waited patiently then formed a line. Bruce and Stevie got to their feet and followed the spiders.

"We'll be going to Selena now "said Stevie to Bruce.

When they got to Selena's rock pool, Stevie took the key out of the pouch.

Selena's face appeared from the rock pool and said"Throw the key in the rock pool". He did as he was told.

Suddenly there was an explosion of light, dust from the cave rose up in the air making it difficult to see.

Bruce terrified let out a miaow and hid behind Stevie. Dust went in their eyes burning their eyeballs, when they looked at each other they were both covered. A white light covered the cave.

A ghostly vision appeared before them. It was Selena.

"Thank you" she said to Stevie. Appearing younger. The wrinkles appeared to have gone. She was now very tall, and straight backed and said "I cannot thank you enough".

Stevie smiled.

"I owe a great debt to you Stephen. I can help my people before it is too late and they are completely destroyed".

She was transforming at a great speed. Her hair was now red falling on to her shoulder in wavy tresses. Her eyes were changing a vivid green. She was majestic looking woman dressed in a white gown. The pair gazed at her in awe.

Stevie finally said "Can you tell us where Fergal is? – we lost him and will Bruce be alright now"?

"Why should I not be?" asked Bruce puzzled.
Selena ignored his question, and touched Bruce's shoulder.
"Ouch" said Bruce. A burning pain went through him.
Collapsing in a heap on the ground, and gazing angrily at Selena he began to mutter under his breath.

Stevie stopped him "Don't be rude Bruce. She has just saved you – Behave".

"What do you mean" said Bruce to Stevie.

"You were turning into a Mercat. If we had not got to you in time. You would have grown fins, and had to stay underwater".

Bruce horrified looked at his feet. He was shocked to see they were webbed, but slowly disappearing back to striped furry feet.

Relieved he turned to Selena and said "Thank you". But suddenly catching sight of his tail which appeared rat like with no hair on. He screamed.

"It will go back to normal don't worry" said Selena. "You have been very lucky. Stevie found you in time. My spiders were sent to guide you Bruce but you kept going in other directions. They tried to get you to look at your feet. Even nipping your toes, but you didn't look down".

"So that's what that was" said Bruce "I was frightened to look down so didn't. I thought if I swam quickly I would get rid of whatever was biting at my feet".

"Thank you so much – but please tell us where Fergal is"? Bruce asked this but was not sure if he wanted to hear the answer.

"It's not good" said Selena. "He has been captured by Sea Witches. They will take him to Glendowwer for the Feast of Molina which is in two days. My aides have told me a lot of my people have been taken there... Horobbin my friend is there. I will be gathering up my armies and we will then destroy the Sea Witches".

"What's the Feast of Molina? Asked Bruce.

"The Feast of Molina is on the 30 October when all the Sea Witches and Warlock's make their annual gathering to Glenodowwer. It represents the Black Sea War when Gledwyn's ancestors fought against humans and won. Gledwyn uses this it to get more witches to join her armies. The kidnapped children and mermaids and sea life are eaten at the feast. The older humans usually have to wait on the tables.

All the guests will have prepared themselves for this. They will have fasted days leading up to this so it will be a good time to strike, as they will be fairly weak from fasting... I am sorry to say Fergal will have been taken as a delicacy for the feast" said Selena.

Bruce and Stevie looked at each other in horror.
"We will come with you won't we Bruce? " Said Stevie.

"Yes we will "said Bruce. He was no fighter but he would help. Just wanting to help Fergal. He had come with Stevie to get him out of the ocean. It was only fair he did the same for his pal. But the thought was frightening. Selena would have to have plenty of support and be able to gather a vast army, or they would be wiped out.

"Please can you help us rescue Fergal"

"Of course" replied Selena to Stevie "But you must be able to fight. It will be a bloody fight". There was silence.

Selena then added "My sisters will now know I am free now. They will go to Glendowwer with soldiers. We will have to plan our attack. Then rise up against the Sea Witches and take Gledwyn off her throne".

A loud reverberating sound came through the cave, Stevie and Bruce put their hands over their ears. It got louder, and louder until it was almost unbearable.

When it had subsided Stevie saw a mass of spiders which seemed to be getting bigger, and bigger. They were now changing shape, stretching at different angles, until they started to form people. They looked human but for the webbed hands.

"These are my people who too were captured, and turned into spiders. The enchantment has now been broken".

The mermaids and merman looked at each other, and hugged each other. It was a relief to see their loved ones back to normal. There was all ages in the group.

Selena welcomed her people. She explained they would now have to go into battle, but that she was gathering up forces. Then she told them to go to their families and get them prepared for war.

One of her mermen changing from a spider to a soldier was Garth. He had a shock of reddish brown hair, and brown eyes. Broad faced, and not as tall as the other troops he was barrel chested with a reddish complexion.

Standing up he went to Stevie and Fergal and said "Thank you for helping us. We would have been trapped as spiders for ever if you had not found the key to release Selena."

As he was speaking Selena looked into the rock pool and spoke to her sister husband Cassim whose father was Marka, King of the Arabian Seas.

Cassim told her he would send his troops to help her. Her other sister Rosanna would send troops from the Atlantic.

The witches had made a lot of enemies, but they still had their own followers, sea monsters, the Eperviers, who could swallow her armies in one swoop.

They had black witches, and wizards who would join up with them and serpents. There was also the fear the underworld would fight against Selena.

Chapter Nine

Fergal had been taken to the Island of Glendowwer. His hand feathers tied so he could not escape. He had fallen a couple of times. A brutal witch called Hilda had kicked him as he fell. Struggling to get up she had laughed cruelly at him. Fergal and a group of mermaids and mer children were then placed into the lower dungeons. Human children then arrived in the dungeon.

One mermaid Lana had told them they had been betrayed by another mermaid called Nadille. She was a friendly mermaid who had been well liked. She had moved to a big house in Pink Lane. No-one could understand where she had amassed her wealth from. Now they knew. She was a spy for the Sea Witches.

"She will have to move quickly" said Lana "If our people catch her she will be held for trial and then imprisoned". She added "Nadille makes friends with you finds out all about your friends, and family, everything you tell her places them at risk". She started to sob "I have let my family down I have told her about my neighbours and friends. The witches will capture them. There is nothing I can do about it". Tears streamed down her face.

Fergal held her hand. Feeling helpless as her. He too had been betrayed by Nadille. She had told him she would be able to find someone who could open the oysters. Instead there was Sea Witches waiting for him. Kidnapping him had ensured Stevie got away. He hoped he had managed to get the emerald key. Looking around at the kidnapped group. A lot were mer children aged from eight to ten. There were more in shock so held on to the adults who had been taken hostage.

Fergal also recognised some of his captors.

There was the McCarthy twins and Blake. They had not seen him but would recognise him. That worried him. They would want to know where Bruce and Stevie were. There were well known for their brutality. It was not as if he could have flown away. Fergal was also very thirsty. He wondered if they would be fed. From what he had heard they were going to be part of the feast of Molina.

Hilda had laughed on the ship mocking him saying "I will enjoy picking your bones" gleefully pinching areas of fat round the base of his tummy. He had tried not to flinch. He knew she would enjoy his pain. Finally, she had got bored when she didn't get a reaction from him and gone on to bully an unfortunate mermaid.

Fergal had been tied up well, but they hadn't accounted for his long sharp beak which would just about free his wings. Pecking away at the rope. It was a very strong rope. It would take some time...

It was nearly night time. He hoped the witches would not come back. There was a lantern in the dark dungeon which shone on the stone floor. There was a door there. If he untied himself and the others he still would not know what would be behind the door.

There was some other cormorants who had been captured, and some sea gulls. He made friends with them. Maybe they could help. He hoped their wings had not been clipped. Still no time for thinking about that, he thought, so continued pecking at the rope with his huge hooked bill. His long neck had come in use making it easier to reach the ropes tying him.

Bruce and Stevie, however, were having a very choppy time in the fishing boat Selena had told them to get in. The current was high. Sea water kept pouring over the boat into their faces as they rowed. Boats were now all around the sea now. Huge sailing ships, and gigantic sea horses carrying soldiers. There was cannons on the ships.

The whole ocean was alive with mermaids, mermen and other aquatic life. Even whales were joining with Selena and carried soldiers on their backs. The only sea life who would not join the battle were sharks and octopus, but everyone knew they were in league with the witches. News would have got to the witches already.

Stevie and Bruce were given chainmail vests, with tabards over them. It would give them some protection but not much. The boat they shared with mermaids, and cormorants. Everyone took it in turns to row.

A thick white foam came out of the sea in front of them four giant sea horses were leading a white and gold carriage. Selena was seated in the carriage her aide guiding the sea horses along the water. Dressed in silver armour. She had now changed completely from an old woman to a confident warrior woman.

Shoals of dolphins and seals followed the carriage. The chariot now started moving at an incredible speed leaving Bruce and Stevie in a white bubby wake.

The sky was now turning a brilliant red. Birds frightened were flying off in flocks in the opposite direction. It was as if they sensed danger was looming.

Out of the sky came huge black crows, which dive bombed the fishing boat Bruce and Stevie and the mermaids were in. This was a bad sign they would no doubt brings news to the Sea Witches Selena had been freed. The crows circled the small fishing boats. There was hundreds of them dive bombing them.

Some the mermaids climbed into the water to escape the pecking and swam along the boats... The crows would be a warm up before the witches prepared for battle.

More of Selena's soldiers appeared in large sailing ships. The crows continued to dive bomb the small fishing boats. The soldiers fired arrows at them, missing some, but the others falling into the water quickly attracted sharks.

The crows screeched like wailing sirens. One grabbed Stevie's fair hair with his beak and attempted to go for his eyes. He whacked it with an oar. It fell into the water and was immediately eaten up by an eagerly awaiting shark. The sharks were now too pre-occupied with the bodies of crows falling into the water killed by soldiers. The water was turning red with the crow's blood.

"At least they are snacking on them and not us" said Bruce horribly fascinated. Stevie looked away. It was very sickly to look at. Soldiers had continued firing at the crows, eventually the remaining ones flew away...

The boats and ships were a mile from Glendowwer. Now the real battle would now begin.

Fergal was having a terrible time. He could not finish untying the ropes with his beak. The witches and warlocks had arrived, and the dungeons were like a market place. Fergal and the other prisoners were poked, prodded and pinched. One very pretty little mermaid Tia was surrounded by a group of witches. The pulled at her hair, and lifted her arms up checking for any fat.

One had a notebook and appeared to be taking notes. When you looked closely it was a recipe book she was holding.

Tia tried to stop the witches touching her. But it pinched her and she cried out in pain.

Fergal could not stand it any longer, and managed to drag himself over to her. Standing in front of the witch. The witches cackled with laughter. One of them aimed her wand at him. He went flying up in the air landing on the ground a sickening crunch...

"Keep away from me "said Tia "They took away my brother for trying to help me". She tried not to cry when she said this.

Her pretty green eyes misting up. More witches came into the dungeons. Fortunately, the witch bullying Tia lost interest in her, and went to greet them.

Fergal managed to drag himself to her "Don't worry we will get out of here" he whispered. Then added "My friends will be looking for me ".

She smiled at him, but seeing the witches come back kept her eyes firmly on the ground.

The kidnapped group had been placed in the dungeons under the tower of Glendowwer. The floors of the dungeons were made of huge slabs of white stone, and were very cold to sit on. The witches started to section off everyone. Tia was in the same group as Fergal.

All the birds apart from Fergal had their wings strapped down tightly, making it very uncomfortable for them.

Some of the children had told Fergal they had come as far away as London. They had come from orphanages. The managers of the orphanages had sold them to the witches. Harry a small boy of ten had found out what the manager of the orphanage had been up to. Just as he was about run away and tell the police he had been captured.

Another of the children was Phoebe. She was aged thirteen. Her aunt had placed her in the orphanage after her mother had died. Their aunt had taken all her mother's things leaving her with only a few old clothes. She had known about the witches, and wanted Phoebe out of the way. Taking over Phoebe's mother house she slowly squandering all the money left for her... There had been no will. Phoebe's mother had trusted her sister. Phoebe's father had disappeared overseas and never come back. It was believed he had been killed .There would be no-one looking for her.

The witches had chosen the kidnapped children well. Nearly all had a history where no-one would be out looking for them.

A sucking noise from a corner where Fergal's group sat appeared to be coming from Tia. Whatever was it?

Tia looking embarrassed said "It's me if I stay out of the water I lose my fish tail".

Fergal watched in fascination as Tia's tail slowly disappeared .Her thin white legs appeared little by little. Even her pointy ears were changing into small human ones. Her whole body appeared to stretch then go through a stage of getting smaller, and smaller. She was not the only one, other merchildren, and adults began to change into human form.

Stevie, and Bruce, and Selena and her soldiers were now not far from Glendowwer. Selena had captured some Sea Witches going to the feast of Molina. Even being helped by Inca the killer whale and his followers. .. It had been easy to capture the witches. They had been too engrossed in preparing for the celebrations. Selena now had their wands and broomsticks. Useful tools they could use. The broomsticks were tied to the up and a spell placed on them so they could not escape. The captured witches then had an enchantment spell placed on them. . They were then taken by soldiers on a boat to Barry Island. Once there they were imprisoned in a stone fortress...

Huge flocks of seagulls, and cormorants had now joined Selena. They too had lost relatives.

Even a golden eagle called "Rufus" had joined and was now mingling with soldiers. He knew the layout of the tower, and remained by Selena's side. As a young bird he had been taken by the Sea Witches but had managed to escape. That was in the early days before the witches had their dungeons in place. He had been incredibly lucky to escape.

At the moment Selena's luck was in but the crows would have told Gledwyn by now so anything could happen. The whales had captured more Sea Witches in their huge mouths. Even some of the sharks now joining forces... It seemed as if the Sea Witches were having more and more turning against them. The whales had done a great job, and continued searching underwater for witches. But it did have a negative effect sometimes. The huge tidal wave they created in their wake made the ships and boat very wobbly, and took time for those steering them to get back on their course.

The sea was also getting black, and much colder coming up to Glendowwer. Almost icy. Stevie stared hard at the dark water, but interest turned to horror.

"Sea Snakes" he shouted. Huge pythons swam along the water wrapping themselves round unfortunate souls in the water who desperately struggled to get free. The snakes swaying figures were getting bigger. Selena was ahead of them.

Bruce and Stevie with the others on the boat would have to help themselves.

One huge snake slithered onto the boat, and increased in size. It wrapped its tail round Stevie's foot as he desperately tried to unravel it. Bruce grabbed an oar and hit it over the head. It huge leathery brown and cream head turned round angrily. Its mouth began stretching as it tried to grab at Bruce, who in turn ducked. The snake dislocated its jaw, and stretched getting bigger. It towered over a trembling Bruce. Stevie grabbing an oar, and proceeded to hit the snake over its body. It angrily turned round to attack him.

It was stopped by soldiers climbing into the boat using bows and arrows to kill it. It was then pushed with great effort back into the sea. The slippery body, and sheer weight made it a difficult task.

More snakes tried to climb into the boat. The small boats were now being attacked by snakes at all sides.

Garth, one of the soldiers fired his musket at them. Sometimes they worked other times they missed. But there were now too many snakes. The soldiers were going to be outnumbered.

Garth shouted across to Bruce from his side of the boat "Don't let them spit in your eyes. The phlegm will make you blind".

Hearing this Bruce ducked from a spitting snake. One of the mermaids managed to get away from the snakes, and swam ahead to Selena.

Selena turned back. Seeing snakes now swallowing soldiers live. She stood up from her chariot, pointed her wand at them and shouted. "Mazaraghan".

The ocean then appeared to roar. The sea rippled. The snakes dropped their prey, and became smaller, and smaller. They eventually turned into water bubbles, and blew far away into the sea.

"It is as I feared" said Selena to Stevie. The witches are already upon on. This is just the start- more will follow". She went back into her chariot. Ahead for Glendowwer other ships following her.

Bruce and Stevie looked at each both wondering "What next?"

Looking around the small boats, and ships you could see some of the soldiers had been badly injured by the snakes. Even Garth had a huge cut on his forehead which dripped blood down his face. Bruce offered him one of his snotty handkerchiefs. Trying not to look disgusted Garth declined. Instead he scooped up sea water and bathed the wound with it. The salty water made it sting, and he tried not to grimace with the searing pain. The other wounded soldiers followed suit.

Garth had been informed by a returning mermaid that Clive the Hammerhead shark had been captured by a shoal of blue whales. This was a relief he had killed many of the mermaids.

Also Nadille the mermaid had been captured. She would now face trial. . She would appear before Omar the Judge. A large monk seal. . There was so much evidence against her. It would not be a good outcome for her.

A half a mile off Glendowwer it was now strangely quiet. A white mist had gathered round the tower, making it difficult to see. The mist was now engulfing all the boats and ships. It appeared to wrap round them like huge white bony fingers. The temperature dropped and now it was freezing cold.

Huge granite rocks lead the way to Glendowwer. They were like something out of a prehistoric age gone by. The moon was now very low shining bright yellow.

Garth came up to Stevie, and Bruce and gave them what looked like a white chalk dust. He also handed them sheathed knives, and bow and arrows on straps which they placed round their shoulders saying "Cover your faces and bodies with this chalk dust. This will give you a small amount of protection from the witches, and warlocks and the Eperviers. " Everyone did as he said.

Bruce paled at the thought of the Eperviers... Remembering terrible stories of them from crew members on ships. How could they be a match for sea monsters?" he thought.

"How does the powder work" asked Stevie.

"It is a healing powder if the witches aim their wands at you the spells should bounce off you. But you will later feel pain. Also, the protection is short lived. The powder only works for a couple of hours after that time it stops working".

Selena was ahead with her soldiers now using her power to open the huge gates. A roar sounded in the air which was deafening.

"Eperviers!" someone shouted.

Chapter Ten

An enormous monster lumbered towards Selena. She did not back off aiming her wand at the creature. It appeared to shrink. Another one appeared, and she did the same again. A third appeared but she seemed to falter, stumbling, getting out in time as the huge creature tried to grab her with its long talons.

Gathering herself together she lay on the ground, and once again she aimed her wand at the creature. It disappeared into the air. But the act appeared to her sapped her strength. She was helped up by one of her soldiers. She looked exhausted. Dressed in full armour she had taken off her helmet and started taking deep breaths.

Bruce and Stevie had dragged their boat up to the sands of Glendowwer and were now not far from Selena.

"Some of you" said Selena to her soldier "Will be hurt in battle. You must be strong. You are all helping your families. I will protect you as much as I can... My sisters will be here shortly. If we do not destroy them they will be no more sea life left. This is our future and our only hope".

Her vivid eyes glanced sharply at those around her. She then smiled. "Come on let's get the job done". Her words full of strength. . She then placed her helmet back on.

Bruce and Stevie had now caught up with her and went with Garth and his men. The next question in their thought "What will the witches send next"?

Back in the dungeons Fergal had not slept at all. The witches had finally gone. The prisoners had been given water and plenty of food to fatten them up. The water had been a blessing. Fergal had been so thirsty.

He had been going through his tail feathers, looking for a suitable sharp feather which could pick locks. Then attempted to pluck an extremely thin tail feather. It would not budge, and made him wince at each attempt. Finally, he found a feather suitable for the job.

"Harry" shouting to his new found friend in the dungeons. "Pluck this one out for me will you?" It was still stuck tightly in his rump. Fergal pointed at the one he wanted pulled out Harry gave it a tug and pulled it out.

"Ouch "Ouch "screeched Fergal his eyes watering...

"Keep the noise down you lot" shouted the magpie jailor from the other side of the door. Not even bothering to look up.

He was busy enjoying his worm pie.

"Why do you want this feather Fergal? "Asked Harry.

"It might get us out of this cell if I can pick the lock with it".

He bit away at the feather making it into a very sharp point. Using spit to help bend it. After much biting it started to resemble a key. The rest of the prisoners started to get excited, but an angry glare from Fergal soon quietened them down.

He had also bitten through the rope tying his wings. He untied Harry, and everyone began untying everyone else. The relief of being untied was wonderful. Everyone nursed their sore wings, and wrists.

Fergal peered through the keyhole of the dungeon door. The magpie jailor had fallen asleep after his huge meal. He looked a horrible sight. His head had fallen to one side on the chair he sat on. Spit oozing down his beak, his uniform, grey trousers and white shirt all stained with food. On his head a grey cap. His shirt pink stained with the sticky pie dinner he had just eaten. On the floor was half eaten starling sandwich.

It was a horrible sight but it reminded Fergal of Bruce. He laughed silently to himself. In his bones he felt that Stevie and Bruce were safe. He imagined the witches would want to keep Bruce as a pet if they caught him he thought. But Stevie would be a different matter. He would be lunch. A plan slowly came to him as he observed the magpie.

"Hey Harry I've got a plan". He whispered back to him "The jailors a magpie. What do you think magpies like best in the world"?

Harry looked puzzled "Why something shiny of course" said Fergal answering his own question. "We need to get the key off the jailor. This feather I have made as a lock is still no good for opening the door". The other prisoners were now listening intently.

"Has anyone got anything shiny - jewellery perhaps?" asked Harry.

Tia took off a little heart shaped green seahorse pendant she had on. Some of the others had coins in their pockets. One of the other mermaids dropped a topaz ring in. Finally there was a pile of glistening coins, and jewellery on the dungeon floor.

"Right" said Fergal quietly "Let's give the magpie some glitter for his collection. This is the plan". Everyone listened.

"Let's hide some of the jewellery round parts of the dungeon. Make him think we have far more than we have. Make sure an odd one is visible Magpies have great eyesight so he will spot anything shiny right away. Who will be the actor?

We need a volunteer someone to say the words the magpie will want to hear?"

Tia said "I'll do it".

"No" said Phoebe. "Let me I have a much louder voice Tia's voice is too softly spoken".

She had a point Tia whispered as she spoke but her voice appeared loud to the rest of the prisoners. So it was agreed Phoebe would be the actress. She would be a very good actress. Tia was secretly relieved she was hopeless at lying and was worried she might let everyone down

They group quickly placed pieces of jewellery round the dungeon floor. They had been lucky their jewellery had been no interest to the Sea Witches. They seemed more interested in slavery and their stomachs at the moment.

So Phoebe started talking loudly speaking about her late uncles family business all made up. She was very good. Then started on about the family heirlooms.

"All I have now are the pieces I have hidden here and they are worth a small fortune".

Fergal peered through the dungeon keyhole and watched the magpie jailer. The magpie hearing the loud voice awoke with a start kicking his starling sandwich further along the ground. But now the magpie seemed uninterested in the sandwich. Too busy listening to the voice on the other end of the dungeon door.

As he listened Fergal could the bird getting more and more interested. The greed showing in his eyes was now plainly obvious. He rubbed his feathers down one side of his body.

"Jewels - Did he hear the word "Jewels"? The magpie thought the children were orphans. Maybe some had come from rich families. If there was jewels in there he would get them and still keep the prisoners for the feast of Molina". He had to get the prisoners to trust him. Scratching his chin. A plan came into his mind. They would want to be set free. He would barter the jewels for their freedom. Then he would double cross them and keep the jewels. The witches would never know. That's when he could fly away and start a new life.

"Right" he thought he would have to be on his best behaviour for those stupid prisoners. Proceeding to brush the crumbs off his chest he stood up.

Fergal immediately got away from the keyhole and stood behind the cellar door. He had found a piece of sackcloth which would do the job.

Unlocking the dungeon door the magpie walked in. All the other prisoners had quickly placed the ropes loosely round their wrists. The magpie did not appear to notice this or that Fergal was on the other side of the door. The cormorant was thin, but still had to breathe in as the magpie came through the door.

"What's the commotion?" asked the magpie smiling pleasantly at the group. "Don't be afraid I was concerned about you all".

Phoebe answered. "We are all frightened about tomorrow - we don't know what's happening".

"Don't be afraid" said the magpie. "I am a prisoner as much as you. I need money to make a fresh start to get away from the Sea Witches".

"We wish we could help you" said Phoebe pleasantly.

"I heard what you said "said the magpie. Phoebe feigned shock horror.

The magpie responded quickly "I will do a deal with you. Give me the jewels, and I will leave the dungeon door unlocked. How you escape is up to you. I will not tell the witches because I will be taking off as well". Phoebe and the group pretended to discuss this.

The magpie watching the group had not realised Fergal was not there. Too interested in looking for the jewellery, his sharp eyes caught sight of glistening coins under bits of sackcloth. Getting excited. His beak began to quiver. Trying to not make it too obvious as his beak was now wet with saliva.

He said "What a pretty little mermaid you are" earnestly patting Tia's tiny head much to her disgust with his sticky feathers.

But she did not move away from him, but was relieved when Phoebe replied "How can we trust you?"

"You have to trust me otherwise you will all be meals for the witches" said the magpie bluntly hoping it would fill them with terror.

He had seen the coins. But where were the jewels he had heard about? He then drooped his head sadly hoping they would feel sorry for him.

"I have a family" he said. All lies but he hoped they would be gullible enough to believe it. "I haven't seen them for two years I need money to help them. We could all help ourselves. Give me the jewels and I will set you free".

He came further into the dungeon still engrossed while he was talking in looking for the jewels. The group had hidden them under their feet. It made their feet tickle. Sharp edges cut into their feet but they had to bear it. They hoped it was not for long.

"I hate the witches" said the magpie. That bit was true but they did keep him well fed. But it was difficult getting time off. He was quite a lazy bird. This job had suited him fine, but there was also room for improvement. If he could be rich and do nothing for the rest of his life well that would be just fine.

The children and cormorants all looked at each other. Harry said in fake innocence to the group "I think he's telling the truth we should tell him where the jewels are". The others all nodded in agreement and quickly Tia handed the magpie a jewelled head band she had under her hair.

The magpie was so fascinated by this object he failed to see Fergal creeping up behind him

The sackcloth was placed firmly over his head. It completely covered his small frame. The magpie realising what was happening made loud clucking noises. They were drowned out by the heavy cloth.

Fergal ripped the top of the cloth with his sharp beak. The magpie's irate face came into view so he quickly bit of sack cloth into a makeshift gag. This was placed firmly over the magpies' beak. He was then held down by the others.

Opening the dungeon door Phoebe went into the jail room and came back with rope. This was tied round the magpie's waist. He was now placed firmly on the dungeon floor. .

The cormorants' were thoroughly enjoying the magpies rage. He had poked, prodded them, and pulled out their tail feathers. Now he would see what it was like to be a prisoner.

The magpie was dumbstruck. How could he not have seen what they were up to?

The magpie's keys were removed from him, and the prisoners went out of the dungeon door. There was a large pitcher of water which everyone drank from quickly. With everyone getting refreshed Fergal and the other cormorants' kept watch.

The dungeons appeared to be split into two blocks. There would be other prisoners they could release. The next level may have witches on. They would have to use guile to outwit them.

The group crept up to the next level Fergal peeped round the corner there was a group of crows playing cards. They were too busy arguing with each other to notice the group quietly go to the next level.

Prisoners might be on this level, but would it be too risky to do anything? They would have to come back later them thought Fergal disappointedly. The stairs were very steep. The cormorants found it easy as they half flew up. One cormorant Connor flew all the way up. He did a quick check and beckoned them all up.

The next floor had passage ways they could hide in, which would be useful. There was a strong cooking smell which did not smell very nice. Fergal crept nearer to the pungent room.

The others stayed in the shadows. He quietly turned the handle of the door. Peering in he could see nothing it was full of smoke.

As he tried to back out a strong force dragged him back in. The door shut behind him, enclosing him into the spiralling darkness.

Chapter Eleven

Selena had now arrived with her troops to the entrance of the tower. There were no witches there. It was very odd. Everyone had already climbed over the granite rocks leading up to tower. Rufus the eagle was now perched on a slab of rock. Stevie looked around anxiously. That's when it started. A loud clapping in the sky. It was if a million birds had fluttered their wings.

"Look out" shouted Garth. "Witches".

They appeared to be witches of all shapes, and sizes hovering in the sky. They began to swoop down on the group.

Garth picked up his bow and arrow and starting firing at them. He hit one on the forehead, and she came hurtling down from the sky. Landing with a screech on the ground. Other soldiers started firing at them.

A bony hand grabbed Stevie. As he tried to free himself, a sand witch came out of the ground. Its alabaster skin shone against the sparkling sand. The eyes were flaming red, and she had a long red tongue hanging out of her mouth.

Stevie was now being pulled into the sand by the two sand witches. The chalk they had covered his body did not seem to help. Garth fired arrows at them. One witch fell to the ground, but the other sand witch clung on to Stevie. Bruce grabbed at the witches hair. As she turned to grab him, Garth aimed his arrow into her back. She fell back into the sand.

Bruce then helped Stevie out of the sinking sand. But more sand witches came out of the sand. They were going to be outnumbered. A sand witch grabbed Bruce's tail. He let out a cry of pain. Stevie grabbed Bruce's tail, and pulled with all his might to get the witches grasping hands away from him. The final pull dragged Bruce away from the ravenous creature.

Bruce and Stevie managed to climb on to large rocks, finding a large one, quite high up. It was horrifying to watch. Soldiers were being sucked into the sand by the witches. Garth was once again fighting two witches at a time.

Bruce and Stevie picked up loose rocks and began firing them at the witches. Garth winded one witch with an arrow, but a second witch grabbed his shoulder, a third was about to aim her wand at him when one of Stevie's rocks hit her in the back. She turned round to him in a violent rage screeching. Aiming her wand at him, she fell to the ground sinking into the ground just as a soldier's arrow killed her.

Garth managed to fend off the final witch attacking him. She took off on her broomstick and disappeared into the sky.

Selena was busy tackling a group of witches .One of them aimed her wand at her.

The spells bounced off Selena. It was almost as if she was invincible. Pressing her amulet to her chest as a large circle of witches approached her. She chanted some words. They went flying up in the air. Far into the sky, disappearing into pin pricks into the sky. Other witches seeing this took off in fear. The sand witches left, she aimed her wand at. Circles of fire appeared around them. The witches screaming sank into the sand.

Selena then went further down the beach rescuing soldiers who were sinking into the sand. The last witch was killed by Garth's arrow. They had won this battle.

The golden sand bubbled as it took away the witches. The only thing Selena had kept were their broomsticks. These were lined up in rows, and she chanted words to them. They became docile, and obeyed her every command.

The sand witches had now gone, but out of rock crevices appeared goblins. Tiny creatures. Devious, and cunning. They stabbed with tiny knives at the soldiers, any points they could reach, mainly ankles and feet. Shouting. The soldiers jumped in the air. Trying to catch the goblins was useless. The goblins went at the speed of light, ducking and dodging the soldiers.

The tiny figures grinned evilly at the soldiers. Ugly creatures with triangular shaped faces, pointed chins and long noses. Long trailing brown hair hung down their tiny shoulders.

They were dressed completely in a grey type of sackcloth, with big leather belts round their waists. Attached to their belts were tiny swords.

Selena seeing the commotion these tiny figures were causing summoned six of the sand witch's broomsticks, and gave orders to them. They rose in the air, and chased after the hapless goblins. They ran away but the broomsticks continuing to chase the little figures.

Finally the group lost sight of the goblins who were now at the other end of the beach. This had not been good for Selena as she had used up a lot of her strength, and was getting quite weak...

Bruce's tail was in agony from the witch pulling it. Stevie's arms hurt blood had started to come from a wound which started to appear. He wiped it as best as he could with a handkerchief. All the others who had put the powder on were now feeling pain.

Selena had found broomsticks hiding behind rocks. Fearing for their lives they shrieked in high falsetto wails.

"Obey me" Selena shouted at them "I will not hurt you".

The broomsticks calmed down. Listening intently to her they had been badly treated by the witches. Some had burn marks where witches had punished them for minor misdemeanours. The broomsticks flew meekly to Selena's feet. She chanted a few words. They would now obey her commands.

The group climbed up the rocks, up a grass verge leading up to the tower. More soldiers arrived, to Stevie and Bruce's horror Ethan walked up the beach with some of his men. Just as they were about to say something to Selena. She ran down to shake Ethan's hand warmly.

Bruce his whiskers twitching whispered to Stevie "We're in for it now".

"No, you won't be" said Selena turning round to them. Her bright eyes had once again missed nothing. "Ethan, is a dear friend. While I have been imprisoned. He has been fighting the cause and secretly been against our enemies".

Ethan turned to Stevie and Bruce and smiled. "I never thought I would see you both again. I thought the witches would have got you both. What happened to your friend Fergal"?

"We think he's in the tower" said Stevie. He was amazed. Who would have thought Ethan was on their side. Bruce as usual was having none of it. He avoided Ethan's gaze.

Seeing Bruce's discomfort he spoke to Stevie and Bruce saying "We always thought it was humans that had destroyed our homes, and killed our families. How we hated them – we have since found out it was the Sea Witches who have committed these evil deeds... Selena tried to help our families."

As he spoke the golden eyes seemed to relive some distant horror. "We are now her soldiers – but you two have been marvellous freeing her- who would have thought a kid, a cat and cormorant could do so much". He let out a laugh and shook their hands much to Bruce's annoyance.

"I'll forgive you for putting a spell on us –you little monkeys. But not the bad head you gave me when I woke up."

"How did you find out? Bruce asked.

"A seagull told us that he saw you getting into the boat. He is a friend of ours –also you were the only ones missing Do you know I was trying to protect you from the snake Stevie. That's that is why I took you to back to the cabin. I could not risk the snake coming back and finishing you off". He looked sternly at Stevie

It all made sense now. Ethan had stopped him being eaten by the snake on the ship. How frustrated Ethan must have been with him... Stevie embarrassed but just relieved he was a friend shook his hand.

"The McCarthy twins I knew were spies for the Sea Witches" said Ethan. "But I had to see what they were up to. They have been involved in the slavery. They left the ship in a boat. I think they may be in the tower with the witches ".

The group looking around them. There was now no other witches in sight. They had now reached a small gate leading up to the tower door, but it was shut tight.

"We will have to force the door open" said Ethan.

"Not necessary "said Selena touching her amulet... The huge door opened.

The group entered. But as she came through the gates she collapsed to the ground.

As Ethan went to help her she spoke weakly "I need to rest. I have used too much of my power".

He helped her to sit on the ground. She lay there trying to get her strength back. But within a split second of entering there was thumping noise. Getting louder and louder. Ethan recognised it immediately.

"Epervier" he shouted.

Everyone looked where he was looking. Selena tried to use her wand, and pointed it at the creature but it failed to heed to her command. She could only look helplessly as the enormous creature lunged forward, making the ground tremble.

Rufus the Golden Eagle flew round the monsters head as it tried to get to Stevie. Distracted. It swayed its head furiously from side to side. But the brave eagle was swift, and dodged its head. The monster snapped at the bird with its huge razor like teeth. The eye in the centre of the creatures head dilated. It moved its hawk head from side to side.

Garth and Stevie threw rocks at the creature. Ethan then fired a bow and arrow at the creature. The arrows bounced off.

The monster was twenty feet in height. As it swung round at Rufus, its lizard like tail tried to catch him. It then opened its huge mouth. A long black forked tongue came out. It put its head back, and tried to catch the bird with it... Rufus was now getting exhausted, flew lower out of the creature's way. Garth fired arrows at the creature. Its attention was now fixed on Garth. Rufus then escaped as more, and more arrows were fired into the creature's body. But the last arrow Garth fired broke.

The creature seeing this lurched forward picking up Garth by his clothes with its tongue before he could escape. The others could only look on helpless. Garth wriggled as it wrapped its tongue round him trying to crush him.

Just as it was about to put him into its mouth, he managed to free himself. He stabbed it with his sword... With a further thrust he cut at the tongue. The Epervier screeched in pain dropping its victim.

Garth fell to the ground. Just as the creature raised itself up to attack him again. Selena appeared pointing her wand at it. It immediately turned it into stone.

Looking at the direction she was pointing at there was another Epervier. This too was turned to stone.

Stevie helped Garth to his feet. He was badly bruised from his fall, but had not broken any bones.

They were now at the door of the tower. Opening the huge oak door they were met with vast tunnels. Ethan asked Selena how she was. She was very pale.

Shaking her head at him she answered "I'm fine I just needed a rest. Come on let's get on with the job in hand".

Ethan showed concern but she glanced at him coldly. This was enough for Ethan to know he should say no more about it.

Chapter Twelve

"I know the basics of the tower," Ethan said. "A cormorant managed to escape and has sketched a basic blueprint of it. The lower ground are the prisons. They are guarded by crows and magpies. There might be witches disguised as snakes so watch out."

Stevie didn't say anything. He was remembering his encounter with the snake on the ship shuddering inwardly.

Everyone now went into groups. Bruce went with Stevie and Garth, and two of the soldiers. Ethan went with some other soldiers. Selena went with Rufus, and more soldiers and mermen.

Bruce the smallest of the group crept into a door on the side of the entrance. He found a lone magpie tied up. Trying hard not to lick his lips at this tasty morsel. He beckoned to the others.

Stevie unbound the birds gag and said. "We will not harm you ".

The magpie was gulping with fear. "Where are the prisoners"? The bird gaining its composure started speaking "The mermaids and children escaped with the cormorants.

They tied me up and I was left in this state." The magpie tried to move his flattened down wings. Adding angrily, "I hope the witches have caught them and eaten them. Do you know I have been tied up for at least an hour?" Realising he had said the wrong thing to the angry group he gulped.

"Well we are very sorry to hear of your ordeal," said Stevie with pretend concern, "but we are going to have to leave you tied up a little longer so you don't warn the witches." With that he replaced the gag back on the furious magpie. The magpie tried to fly up at him without success, realising it was hopeless it gave up cursing under its breath.

They were so busy talking amongst themselves they did not see the door open. Bruce was the only one who heard it and turned round.

A dozen crows flew into the dungeon. They flew at the group faces. Garth fired a bow and arrow at one then at another one. The crows started to fall down. The other two soldiers aimed their bow and arrows. The crows then landed on the ground in a black feathered mass.

The group left the dungeon cautiously looking around, checking each door as they went along. Coming on to the second floor of the tower they arrived at one of the vast kitchens.

There was a buzzing noise. A group of witches flew at them. Ducking, Garth fired a further arrow at one that was trying to claw his face. He grabbed her wand and aimed it at her. The spell she was placing on him now bounced off him and went on her. She grew smaller turning into a white rat and scuttled away.

Another one rounded on Bruce, her long black claws grabbing tufts of his fur. He scratched her with his claws. Finally he sank his teeth into the tough smelly flesh. Screeching, she released his fur.

Quickly, he grabbed her wand, throwing it into the burning cauldron in the room. The witch flew to retrieve it but was shot done by arrows by one of the soldiers. She fell motionless to the ground. Garth and the soldiers then managed to shoot the rest of the witches down with their bow and arrows.

But one witch remained and grabbed Stevie by the hair. This was a much older witch with long grey hair. A fearsome looking creature she bared her teeth at him. She dodged the arrows fired at her by Garth and the soldiers. The yellow eyes shone evilly at Stevie.

"I shall so enjoy eating you boy" she hissed at him. "Barbecued boy lovely- boys tend to taste a bit like roast beef" she laughed.

Dragging him closer to her with an iron grip. Stevie could not free himself. The claw like hands came closer to his eyes. He had to use all his strength to drag the claws away from them. The arrows bounced off her from Garth. She was a much stronger witch.

While she was wrestling with Stevie, Garth swiftly nipped in and dragged her broomstick from beneath her. Shrieking she turned round trying to grab it back. Stevie took this opportunity to turn round and grab her hair. Garth then raced to the bubbling cauldron and threw the broomstick in. The witch screamed, and cursed Stevie raking his face with her pincer like claws. Garth and Stevie managed to overpower her, finally pinning her down.

A footstool placed upside down was held over her. The wand she had was also thrown into the cauldron. Unable to move the witch lay trapped on the ground in rage. Garth then tied her feet with rope he found near the kitchen table. Stevie had to hold the footstool firmly so she could not wrestle it from him. With her long bony feet tied they half prised the footstool off her. The witches claws tried to scratch at them but with two people fighting her they overcame her. She was then wrapped up in rope. Stevie's face was already bleeding quite badly from her claws.

Garth took the witches legs, and Stevie took her arms. Bruce opened the large cream pantry facing the kitchen table. The witch was unceremoniously pushed in. She uttered curses at them as the door was shut on her. There was a noise coming from inside there. Peering in the red eyes of another witch stared back at them. She did not appear to have a broomstick or a wand so would be harmless. The door of the pantry was then slammed shut again on the cursing pair.

Locking the door Garth and Stevie were breathless. They looked at each other with relief. There was now no other witches in the kitchen.

Bruce appeared with a jug of cold water, and damp cloth and proceeded to wipe Stevie's deep cut on his face.

"Ouch" said Stevie. The cut was very sore. It took a while for the bleeding to stop. The others guarded the kitchen door.

"Don't worry It'll heal" said Bruce "Come on let's get out of here. This room gives me the creeps".

As they went to go out of the door Bruce spotted rows of meat hook. Dead cormorants hung on them. Not wanting to look at the dead birds he said "Do you think?" he did not finish the words. A lump formed in his throat. Stevie knew what he was thinking.

"I don't know" said Stevie his voice wavering.

They did not want to utter the words "Fergal". But Bruce decided to be brave and looked at the rows of dead cormorants. Looking at them carefully. A wave of nausea came over him.

"None of them are Fergal" said Bruce." Fergal had a scar on his beak. I can't see any of them having that."

He was interrupted by a banging noise came from the floor. Stevie lifted up the rug where the noise was coming from. It was a trapdoor. Garth and the soldiers stood by the trap door. Stevie opened it, peering in.

Down below pasty white faces peered out. It was Tia, Phoebe, Harry and other prisoners. The soldiers helped the children out. After them came Fergal. They were all dazed and wobbly. It had been a tight fit.

Stevie and Bruce just stared at Fergal stupidly.

Finally, Stevie broke the silence "We thought you had been killed Fergal". It was hard not to cry with relief.

Stevie gave Fergal a bear hug. Bruce then charged at Fergal knocking him down in his excitement.

"I suppose you were too fishy to eat" he said to Fergal.

"I'll ignore that remark "said Fergal sombrely. He was in no mood for jokes no matter how pleased was to see them. "Our friends the cormorants didn't make it" said Fergal trying not to cry. He beckoned to them the rows of dead cormorants in the room.

Changing the subject he introduced them to his new friends. Garth shook Fergal's hand. The children looking from Bruce to Stevie to the soldiers still in a state of shock.

"Ethan's here" said Stevie.

"What!" said Fergal?

"It's alright he's with Selena. He's been helping her. Would you believe he had been trying to help us"!!! Stevie replied.

"What did he say about us putting him to sleep" asked Fergal.

"He wasn't very happy but he was laughing. We won't be murdered if that's what you are thinking" Stevie grinned.

They were interrupted by Garth "Come on "he said "Move on".

Beckoning to one of the soldiers he said "Keep the children by the boats they will be a lot safer than where we are going. If you see any trouble go without us but make sure they are safe". Speaking firmly. The soldier nodded in reply.

"I am not going" said Tia. I want to stay with Fergal".

"It's too dangerous" said Garth. But Tia, and Phoebe refused to go and would not be budged.

"Fine but stick close together, you can stay with us but the rest of the children go with our men "said Garth exasperated. None of the other captured children wanted to stay and went willingly with the men. Gath did not have time to argue in this matter.

"Fine but stick close together. Run away if any witches come near you or throw anything you can at them".

Tia nodded and held Phoebe's hand.

They went up the next level. It was very steep. Tia touched the rail going up the flight of stairs. Her hand became immediately sticky. Horrified, she looked at her hand. It was covered in slime. There was slugs starting to cover the rails.

"Ugh "said Tia and Phoebe in unison.

White slime was beginning to fall off the rails in streams. Tia tried to wipe it off her hand but it stuck.

"We'll get some water and wipe it off later" said Bruce.

"We will be approaching the laboratory shortly if my blueprint is right "said Ethan appearing from one of the rooms.

He was busy scanning his blueprint of the tower and said "I thought I'd better check on you all"

Stevie said "We have two witches locked in the pantry. As you can see we found Fergal and some new faces. They were under a trap door".

Ethan looked at Tia and Phoebe.

"Don't be afraid" he said "Be brave. We will protect you. Garth. Why were these children not taken back to one of the ship? It is not safe for them"?

Garth replied nervously "All the other children we found went back to the ship. These two refused to go".

Ethan sighed at the children "It is too dangerous for you".

The little mermaid Tia tear stained said "The witches took my brother Christopher away. I heard him crying. Then it stopped. I don't know where he is. Please find him. I won't go until you find him".

Ethan looked round the room they were now walking into. There was many cupboards. But they could be rooms behind them.

"Christopher "he shouted. He shouted it several times. Tia joined in but no-one replied. They then went silent trying to hear a muffled voice. But there was no sound. They opened all the doors, and cupboards. He was nowhere to be found.

"They might have taken him to the next room" said Ethan "We will search them. We will no doubt find more prisoners as we go along".

A squeaky voice piped up "Let me help you I know the layout of the place"

The voice appeared to be coming out of Phoebe's pocket. Phoebe pulled her pocket back. There was a small wand with dark brown eyes gazing at them.

"I could not burn her "said Phoebe helplessly "She begged me not to. I think she will help us. I found her in the kitchen".

"But can we trust her"? Ethan replied his eyes glinting. The small wand looked worried

"I just want to be free". It shouted at them. "If I help you. Just let me go and not force me to work for you. I will help you find the little boy.

"I am not sure about this". Ethan looking suspicious.

"Please don't hurt her" said Phoebe clutching her pocket so tightly.

The little wand was nearly squashed by this action, and piped out "Let me out"

She pulled the pocket back open again to let it breathe.

"We will free you if you help us but if you double cross us. You will be firewood- Understand" said Ethan growled at the trembling wand.

It nodded back at him saying. "I'm not a spy. I just want to go home".

Home for the wand had been at a wooden house in the

GreNadilles. The wand had loved the family it lived with. But it had been stolen by a travelling salesman, and sold to Sea Witches. That is when its nightmare had begun. Bought by a witch.

The witch had used it as a scratching post to scratch her neck. The flaky skin on the witches back would sometimes touch the wands face. It would have stifle its revulsion.

Breaking into the wand thoughts Ethan asked..." If you are going to help us your first job will be this. Can you look in the next room and tell us what is in there"?

The wand nodded to Ethan. It flew out of Phoebe's pocket. Rising into the air. It flew to a door .The group followed it trying to be as quiet as possible. It disappeared through the door.

"Well" thought Stevie "that will be the last we see of it. It will warn the witches". It came out a few seconds later.

"I didn't warn the witches Stevie" .It said sulkily "A promise is a promise. There are three witches, and a warlock- but they have been drinking ale" said the wand "They will not be prepared for you. Act now if you want to attack them"

"Right" said Ethan" I will go first they might recognise me and think I'm one of them. Stay here I will shout for you". He beckoned to the others. Ethan opened the grey wooden door. It creaked as he went through. The others slid in line to the side of the door so when it opened they could not be seen.

There was a loud noise, then screaming within minutes of Ethan entering the door they heard him shout "Now".

Ethan was fighting a confused warlock. Two other witches were about to aim their wands at him. The wand chanted at one of the witches wands. It flew up in the air coming side to side with Phoebe's wand.

The other witch was shot with arrows by Garth as she turned to face her attacker. Phoebe picked up some sack cloth and threw is at her. The sheet blew into her face. Stevie and Bruce then grabbed her arms, and she was thrown to the floor. Phoebe's wand then aimed itself at the witch and she was tied up with rope. Furious, and screaming she spat at them.

The wand flew higher up and chanted a few more words. The spit turned direction and went into the witches face.

"I'll burn you alive" The witch shrieked. Spit oozed down her face.

The other witch picking herself up tried to escape quietly out of the door, but was caught by one of Garths' soldiers. Phoebe's wand with a chant tied her up.

The warlock was the only one left in the room. Ethan had cornered him, and held the dagger to his throat. The warlock was then tied up, his wand taken from him. It was in a total confused state. His reactions had been very poor. Ethan had been lucky. If the warlock had not been supping the ale from the vast cauldron he may not have overcome him.

With the last of the witches, and the warlock trussed up the group looked round the laboratory. There seemed to be small doors on each side of the boiling cauldrons of ale.

Opening one of the doors Stevie was met with a gigantic pair of scales. A small boy fast asleep on them.

"Christopher" screamed Tia.

But he was in a deep sleep, only waking with the help of the wand chanting a few words. Sleepy eyed he rubbed his face and looked at Tia. Realizing who she was as he was lifted off the scales he fell in to her arms.

"Christopher is my brother" said a breathless Tia. Christopher at first had difficulty walking. The cramp wore off. He then held her hand as the group went out of the laboratory.

Ethan turned to the wand now back in Phoebe's pocket. "You have been a great help to us after all" he said smiling. "What is your name"?

The wand replied "Meena."

"You are now one of us. If you choose to leave us we will let you go" said Ethan expecting the wand to now go.

The wand looked at all the group one by one. The tiny face screwed up. "I think I will stay with you" then she added. "Well until you have won the war that is". The wand gave a gentle smile.

"Let's go then "said Ethan relieved. The wand would be a great help to them if it could go through doors. Coming out of the room they were met by Saros the Rottweiler, two other dog pirates and behind them were more soldiers.

"I knew you would come" said Ethan shaking their hands warmly.

"The McCarthy twins are here" said Saros "They have as we suspected been providing merfolk and children for the witches".

There were further doors on this level. Meena the wand once again went magically into the next room.

She came out within second saying. "Goblins are in there. They are preparing spices for the Feast of Molina. Be careful. Do not be fooled by their size. They have killed many humans in the past".

Ethan slowly opened the door. Swarms of bats flew at the group. The bats were not aiming for the group just trying to get desperately out of the room. The goblins had been throwing them into the cauldrons. The group tore them away from their hair and clothes. The bats then escaped out of the door.

The goblins who had been preparing mixtures in cauldrons rushed at them with their miniature daggers. Garth turned over a vat of uncooked oil, and the oil poured over the ground. The goblins turned to escape. It was too late... They started sliding along the ground. The oil went up to their waists because they were so small. They remained stuck in. It stuck to them like glue.

"Do something Meena?" shouted Ethan.

With that Meena chanted a few words at the hapless goblins. Large barrels appeared and flew over the goblins head trapping them inside.

At the end of the room Tia had been cornered by a young witch. The witch had an olive lumpy complexion and. bulging green frog like eyes. She was much taller than Tia, and held her down with her large plump arms. Her thick brown plait slapped at Tia's face as she pulled her hair, a black and green ribbon was wrapped round the end of it... The weight of her made it impossible for Tia move away from her. The witch smirked nastily at Tia twisting her hair round to hurt her.

"Get away from me" yelled Tia desperately trying to free herself from the witch.

" I have feasted on mermaids like you" came the sickening reply. "I bet when we put you in water we will have better meal though. I am looking forward to tucking into your juicy fish tail"

Tia, with an unknown strength through terror managed to pull herself up from the witch. She grabbed the wand that was now pointed at her, and she threw it away from her. The witch looked back to retrieve it but Tia forced herself up further, and pushed the witch down with all her might. It worked the witch fell over.

Tia with lightning speed raced over to the wand. Grabbing it she pointed it at the witch. Garth came up behind Tia. He took the wand. Then Meena chanted at the wand. It fell to the ground.

The young witch on the ground began screaming hysterically at the group and spat out the words "Wait until my mother finds you. She will skin you alive. You don't know who my mother is and what she will do to you. But if you let me go I will tell her not to hurt you. Save yourselves... Let me go?"

But the group were not in for any bargaining, especially not with a precocious child.

Meena flew in the air and pointed at her. "Look I know who she is she is Larissa. Gledwyn's daughter."

Everyone looked. You could now see something almost toad like about her. The large, bulging eyes, Yellow pitted skin on her arms. She had definitely inherited her father's looks.

Defeated, Larissa began to croak furiously. Garth finding some rope used for tying up meat, with the help of the others tied her hands. Meena then uttered a few words and sent the snarling young witch into a deep sleep. They then placed her on a chair at back of the room. Larissa began to snore, and began making pig like snorts. This made Christopher giggle.

Stevie and Fergal then guided Tia and Christopher out of the room. Nearly out of the door, warlocks flew in creating flashes of blue crackling sparks with their fluorescent robes. Garth was about to fire his bow and arrow when he went flying high up in the air. Banging his head on the ground as he fell.

Scrambling to help him Stevie was hit with a bolt of light to his back, and lay stunned on the ground. Fergal racing to help his friend grabbed Larissa's wand not sure what it would do. Aimed it at one of the warlocks. The cloaked warlock seeing this tried to grab the wand out of Fergal's hand. But Ethan came behind the warlock hitting him with his paw on the back of his head. Half stunned, the warlock tried to get up. Ethan then grabbed his broomstick from under him.

The other warlock escaped out of the door before anyone could stop him.

"He will have gone for help we'll have to go" said Ethan.

They went to Garth, but he was unconscious. No attempts could be made to revive him.

"Take him to the ship" said Ethan to two of the soldiers. They lifted him up and carried him out.

"Will he be okay?" said Stevie still quite wobbly.

"I don't know "said Ethan worried. "We will ask Selena to look at him later. But we have to get going".

Leaving Garth with two of the soldiers the group went to go up the next flight of stairs. Saros stayed behind and went to search other rooms with two of his men for the warlock.

"We will check the room down this side. Once it's clear we will come back" he said to Ethan.

Tia, Christopher, and Phoebe were at the back of the group. Followed behind Bruce as Ethan made his way further up into the tower.

Climbing up the next flight of stairs they could hear a commotion. Musket fire could be heard. Stevie and Bruce and Fergal looked at each other.

"Sounds like our men" said Ethan leading the way.

Coming up the stairs crows came crashing down the stairs, everyone ducked as the crows went crashing past them. The musket fire became louder. One of Selena's soldiers came flying out of a door. Badly wounded he fell to the ground.

Stevie recognised in an instant who the soldier's assassin was. It was one of the McCarthy Twins. Fergal helped the soldier to his feet just as the twin appeared in full at the door.

Seeing Ethan, the dog showed anger. The pink eyes narrowed. He knew he knew he would have to go into battle with him. The heavy sword he held was blood stained. He lifted it in front of him and pointed it at Ethan in a gesture of defiance. Ethan stretched himself to his full height telling the others to keep back.

The soldiers behind him were now also ready for the fight. Seth McCarthy was a dirty fighter. Ethan knew what he was capable of.

"Ethan what a pleasure. I wondered where you had gone- such a disappointment. You have chosen the wrong side. Selena and her troops will lose this battle. Join with us now before it is too late. I will even let you keep little group of misfits if you do" said Seth".

Ethan growled back "Such a kind offer but I prefer to stay with the winning team. You are a traitor to us all. It was the Sea

Witches not the British who destroyed our homes. The witches disguised themselves, and changed shape into British soldiers. Why do you support them? They have taken everything away from us."

Seth ignored him and spat on the ground saying. "That's all lies that Selena has told you. You are a fool Ethan. You will be lying cold in the ground while I am rewarded with gold by the witches. Selena will be dead. Your fight against us will be all for nothing. You have made your choice. You will die and so will all your friends".

With that the pit bull charged at Ethan. His sword swaying high above his head. Ethan however managed to block him. The swords clashed together making a deafening noise. Ethan then proceeded to aim his sword at Seth's left shoulder, but Seth stopped him by stepping aside to his right.

The landing they were fighting on was quite narrow, and when Seth moved he half fell to one side, Ethan seeing this opportunity slashed at his left leg. The pit bull howled in agony.

In a violent rage Seth charged at Ethan with a grappling motion, striking Ethan on his arm with his sword. Ethan pulled himself away before the blade went too deep. But the damage was done. His arm was now bleeding badly.

The pair circled each other, trying to outwit each other with stabbing motions, but they had the same reactions and blocked each other.

Seth then drew back and lifted his sword once again above his head attempting to bring it down on the Rhodesian Ridgebacks head. But this time his movement was jerky. The pain from his leg started to kick in.

Ethan then slashed at Seth's sword with all his strength. The force of this action made Seth's sword bounce out of his hands. The weapon fell to the ground. Ethan swiftly kicked the sword to one side. Stevie with lightning speed grabbed it. Seth pushed his shoulder trying to get the sword, but Ethan pulled Seth to one side. He fell to the ground. The soldiers then kept Seth on the ground with their feet.

"Meena" shouted Ethan". Do your magic".

The wand slid out of Phoebe's pocket. It flew up into the air and swirled round the restrained dog. Meena chanted some very brief words. The pit bull started to yawn. Its pink eyes closing. It rolled on its back falling into a deep slumber exposing its pink belly.

"How long will the spell last?" asked Ethan.
The wand replied "It should be a day at least".

With Seth fast asleep the group went into the room he had just came out of. Stevie and Fergal held the injured soldier by the arms and guided him into a chair. The soldier was deathly pale. Blood was pouring out the side of his hip. Bruce brought water from one of the vast jugs, proceeding to pour it over his hip. But the blood kept flowing.

"Can you not do something to help him?" asked Stevie to Meena.

She replied "I can only calm the wound. I cannot make it go away. My power is not that strong". With that she flew to the injured soldier with a swaying motions directed at him. Out of air came gushes of water which poured off the soldier's stomach and hip. She let the water continue to pour. Only letting it stop when the blood became milky white, then, quick as a flash the water dried up on his body.

The soldier was still weak but managed to speak "Gledwyn has escaped but we are not sure where".

Bruce wrapped muslin round the soldiers wound, patted his shoulder and gave him some ale to sip.

Ethan spoke to the soldier. "Adam, I am sorry but we are going to have to get going. I need to find Selena and see if we can capture Gledwyn. Fergal can you stay with him"? Ethan looked at Fergal. He nodded back he would.

Finding the soldiers musket on the floor Ethan gave it to Fergal and said. "Look there is a key to the inside of the door. It would be advisable to lock yourself in. Selena's followers should be here soon, but it is best not to take chances". Ethan headed towards the door. The group did not follow him. They had eyed the table laden with food.

"Can we not quickly grab a bite to eat"? Phoebe begged "I'm starving."

"Okay but eat quickly" said Ethan.

Everyone raced to the tables. Bruce was already been helping himself. Crumbs of bread hung off his whiskers. Looking guilty he placed cheese, and bread and fruit on a plate and gave it to the injured soldier. Everyone else then grabbed bits of food, eating it quickly and gulping water.

Saros and his two men came into the room. They too helped themselves to food.

"That corridor is clear we have rounded up some goblins and one witch. They agreed to surrender" Said Saros.

Bruce looking at Saros thought anyone with a half mind would surrender to Saros.

Everyone enjoyed the food. No-one however ate the sandwiches. They didn't like to think what was in them. Even Saros ignored them. Meena the wand only ate a piece of pineapple .Her tiny hands coming out of the wand, and cupping the fruit which was huge in her hands.

"Come on" said Ethan wiping his mouth with his huge paw

"See you later" said Bruce looking worried at Fergal.

"Keep safe" said Fergal.

Stevie picked up a piece of broken table leg on the ground. Thinking it could be used as a weapon.

Bruce tied some rope round his middle. He wasn't sure what he was going to do with it but he thought it might be useful. Breaking the ice Tia grabbed Christopher hand with Phoebe.

"Come along," she said imitating Ethan's South African accent. "We have to get going" speaking with such authority it made everyone laugh.

Ethan looked down at the little mermaid and patted her head affectionately.

Coming out of the room they could hear footsteps running and a loud buzzing. It seemed to be coming from the darkened corridor adjacent to the landing. Ethan made the group stand in line. He and Stevie at the front. Ethan with his sword poised. Stevie with the table leg, behind him was Bruce with the frayed rope. The children at the back followed by Saros and his two men.

Ethan's golden eyes squinted. They tried to make out the figure coming out the corridor. There was more footsteps, and they became poised for battle.

Out of the dark came three soldiers, Ethan instantly recognised one of them. It was Glyn, a merman he had met on his travels.

"The area is clear- Selena's here. We have taken this level over". The soldier beamed at the relieved group as he said this.

Glyn was a stocky, pallid faced youth, dressed in pantaloons. On his head was a three tier hat, and he wore a black waist coat, and white shirt. His long brown hair was tied in a long pony tail. Christopher fascinated ventured close. Tia knowing he was going to attempt to pull his pony tail held him back?

"Any news on Gledwyn?" asked Ethan.

"She has escaped. She may be at the top of the tower now. Come with us and we'll take you to Selena".

"What is the buzzing noise?" asked Bruce but none of the soldiers answered.

Following them they walked into a huge open dining hall. It had an enormous table running the whole length of it.
Everything was in a state of disarray. Chairs turned over. Food dripping off the table. Candlesticks and goblets on the floor in

pools of red wine. The wooden floor was caked in squashed food.

At the end of the table was a pulpit, and five pagan statues. Looking closer you could see they were witches. Their evil expressions with turned back lips in snarling expressions making everyone shudder.

"They look so realistic" said Stevie.

"That's because they are. They have been turned into stone" came a voice behind one of the thick black curtains.

It was Selena, still looking as regal as ever, but looking tired.

A flutter of wings made the group look up to the ceiling. It was Rufus the Eagle flying from the ceiling now perching on the table near to her.

"Hello" said Selena smiling at the group.

Tia and Christopher and Phoebe were introduced to her. Tia, and Christopher were in awe of Selena. She spoke gently to them gaining their confidence, and they relaxed.

Ethan mentioned to Selena that Fergal was looking after one of her men, she looked behind them as soldiers came into the room.

She took two of them with her to check on the soldier and returned shortly with Fergal and another soldier saying "I managed to stop the blood flow. But he is weak, he is resting, but he will heal".

Glancing at Tia, Phoebe and Christopher she said to Ethan "These children will have to stay here. We have to move on. The battle is not over. These children will not be safe where we are going". They will have to go back to the room with the injured soldier, and some of my men".

When Tia protested Selena spoke firmly "You will be much safer there child. We will be fighting. We will not be able to protect you". With that she summoned a soldier beside her who took the children back to the room. Tia turned her head to look at the group. Tears filled her eyes and she ran back to Ethan hugging his long legs. It was a touching display. Ethan could not help but be moved by it.

Meena realising she had not been introduced flew out of Phoebe's pocket and flew in front of Selena.

Ethan introduced Meena to Selena, "This is Meena" said Ethan. "She has helped us greatly, and was cruelly treated by the witches"

As if reading her mind Selena spoke to the wand. "You will want your freedom. When all this is over rest assured you shall have it".

The wand gazed up into Selena's eyes staring in stunned admiration at her. "Thank you" the wand replied finally, amazed that the Queen of Mermaids had thanked her.

The loud buzzing started again.

"What is that noise"? Stevie asked.

"Musket fire "replied Ethan. There must be a battle going on the next level".

More soldiers filled the room. One of them said "The sea birds have informed us that Princess Nadalle has arrived on the shores with her men".

Selena's sisters and Louisa her second in command were now here to help in the war. They were getting stronger. More soldiers and mermen appearing on the stairs.

Stevie looking out of one of the tower windows and could see sailing ships landing on the shore. It was annoying as he didn't have a telescope so could not see if they were Selena's men.

"I think "said Saros "that may be our men". He too was straining to see behind Stevie. "Gledwyn and her mother Edna have made a lot of enemies. Some of the soldiers I have been speaking to have said warlocks have now promised allegiance to Selena. But we may have some of Gledwyns followers left. We will have to be very wary".

Ethan shouted to them "Come on we think Edna may be up here. Selena is looking for her. She is Gledwyns mother. We need to stay together if we end up clashing with her. She is far stronger than ordinary witches".

They walked further up into the tower. Ethan ran to get ahead with Saros and Bruce and Fergal. There was now soldiers in front of Stevie and behind him. It was a comfort seeing them all around now.

Hearing a commotion Stevie looked behind him, as soldiers overtook him. At the foot of the stairs were crows fighting. It was a vicious fight. One crow was getting badly pecked by a group of crows.

Stevie clapped his hands, but in doing so lost his balance and fell half way down the stairs. He managed to hold on to one of the stair railings avoiding any serious damage. No one appeared to have heard him.

Realising everyone was now out of sight he struggled up the stairs to catch them up. As he went up he noticed a small door on his right he had not seen before.

Curiosity got the better of him. He opened the door. Peering in there was a long room, with a bed, and side table. But nothing else. Disappointed he went to close the door, but he appeared to fall backwards into it.

Chapter Thirteen

Feeling light headed and disorientated, Stevie thought he must have fainted. Opening his eyes it seemed as if he was in a very warm cave. But when he tried to move he found he could not move his body. It had completely tightened up.

Thinking he must be having some type of hallucination he tried to shout for the others. No sound came out of this mouth. Finding it difficult to breathe. It was almost as if he was slowly suffocating, and could not even scream out.

This was no dream. His ribs were hurting now. He had an urge to massage them but his arms would not move. The air was getting thinner, and he was starting to gulp to try and catch his breath. Struggling to keep his eyes open he was beginning to feel very sleepy.

There seemed to be faint voices... Almost like an echo reverberating round this strange cave. There was noises he could hear that sounded like crackling. The cave seemed to be moving.

His body was now spinning round, and round. He could not stop himself. Pools of water started to fill the cave, coming towards him in torrents. He was now getting very wet. Then he could hear a loud rustling coming from above him. Then something that sounded like a saw. What was going on?

A loud baritone voice broke in "Stevie don't worry we will get you out of this. Hold on" It was Ethan's voice.

The entrance to the cave was opening up. Murky water poured over his head from above him. It filled his lungs. He was finding it difficult to see. There was a horrible smell, like rotting meat and he tried not to gag. But he was feeling more tired, and was about to fall into a deep slumber when he was grabbed by a collection of hands.

He was being pulled upwards and his body was sucked through what seemed like a leathery opening, then a red filmy mass. More hands touched him. He was not caring now. All he wanted to do was sleep. The water had gone very thick. His brain told him this was not water. But what was it?? He could feel cold air now and he had come out of what he thought was the opening of the cave.

He wiped his eyes, and began to see around him. Then he came face to face with Bruce who had his paws to his face looking shocked.

Water was still in Stevie's ears. He could not hear what Bruce was saying. Ethan was beside him with Saros.

Stevie was breathing better. His chest was very sore making him gasp for breath in spurts. Managing to turn his aching head on the landing he could see a gigantic shadow. His sight became clearer, and could make out what it was.

It was a dark green snake. It must have been at least 40 feet in length. A monster. Its body hung over the sides of the railing on the stairs. The width of it was the size of a life boat.

Looking to where its head was he followed the tail up to its neck. It was red, and gaping open. The mouth wide open, as large as his upper body.

It had not been a cave he had been stuck in. He had been inside the body of a snake.

Bruce broke into Stevie's shocked silence "Are you alright?

Stevie still breathless shakily managed to say "Yes. But my ribs are hurting me".

Meena, who had taken root in Ethan's pocket flew towards him. Stevie's shirt suddenly blew open. His ribs were purple, and black. A strong smelling ointment appeared from out of nowhere on to them. He winced in pain.

"This will help you and you might not be in so much pain". As Meena spoke the ointment spread the length of Stevie's chest.

"Ethan and Saros killed the snake" said Bruce to Stevie. His yellow green eyes wide at what had happened to Stevie. Hardly able to believe what had happened... Bruce continued speaking "We thought we had lost you. She must have swallowed you whole without trying to crush you. How you survived in her stomach is a miracle".

"Who is she?" asked Stevie.

"Why Edna, Gledwyn's mother of course" replied Bruce.

They both looked back at the snake which appeared to be getting smaller. Puzzled they watched fascinated. The snake's body had now folded up into a concertina shape.

It slowly disappeared. A figure appeared. A grey haired woman lay on the ground her eyes closed. She was dressed in the black trademark dress, recognisable by the huge yellow curled claw toes on her feet. She was motionless.

"She's dead" said Saros. His tone showing no emotion.

Struggling to speak because his throat now burned Stevie turned to Ethan and Saros and croaked out "Thank you for helping me. I would have been a goner but for you two".

Saros said "You should thank your little friend. He came to look for you, and nearly got eaten by the snake himself. He managed to run back to us. She must have been coming out of hibernation as her movements were slow. Bruce found your shoes. He managed to get away from the snake and ran to us to help you. You had completely disappeared, that's when we knew she had swallowed you. We would not have been able to kill her if she had been in her usual top form".

"Have you dealt with her before?" asked Stevie.

"Oh yes "said Saros bitterly "She killed my brother and father". His dark eyes glinted and he stopped speaking abruptly. With Saros once he had spoken you did ask any further questions, and certainly not about his personal life.

"I was expecting the worst when they cut the snake open" said Fergal joining in the conversation.

More faces appeared more of Selena's soldiers. There were faces Stevie had not seen before.

Fergal patted Stevie's head and asked the question again "Are you sure you are alright"?

"Of course he is stop fussing. You are not his mother" said Saros getting bored with all the displays of emotion "We have to start moving. Once Gledwyn finds out her mother is dead you will really know what fear is" added Saros darkly.

They all started going up the stairs, Bruce helping Stevie get up the stairs. On the next landing was a warlock.

"That's Minerus" said Ethan "Another friend of Selena's."

Selena appeared and started speaking to Minerus. As they

came up the stair you could hear her talking to Minerus. She told him she would go into to what she believed was Gledwyn's bedchamber with some of her men. Minerus was to go to the opposite side of the corridor with his people.

Minerus and his men went into more rooms. Finding more witches and goblins hiding, instead of fighting. They surrendered.

"Swear your allegiance to Selena" said Minerus coldly. He was a very tall grey hair haired warlock, His long beard came all the way down to his stomach. He towered above everyone else. His pale blue eyes missed nothing. Wearing a blue long sleeved tunic over silk peacock blue pantaloons he spoke to the captured witches.

They did not reply so he repeated it "Swear your allegiance to Selena".

The witches and goblins admitted defeat, and did so. He then placed spell on them which meant they were unable to leave the room they were in.

Meanwhile Selena had found now what did actually look like a bedchamber. Very baronial with rich, red, and gold tapestries on the walls. But looking at the wooden carved pictures there were unpleasant fighting scenes which made you look away. They were frightening. There was a gold ornate chair. The cushions were covered in rubies, and pearls no doubt stolen from people when she raided their homes thought Selena grimly.

The huge bed was a white marble monstrosity with carved snakes entwined round the legs. A silk red blanket lay across it. A dragons head painted on the head board. The dressing table was also white marble, with a large mirror. On the dressing table were numerous bottles.

For some reason she could not take her eyes off the ornate dressing table mirror. Peering in it became misty. She then began to understand what was behind it. It reminded her of the rock pool she had been imprisoned in.

Figures appeared through the mist. A middle aged man, and woman, and an old lady appeared before her eyes. They could see her, and stood back with their arms around each other defiantly.

Selena muttered some words and the mirror smashed. The people in the mirror fell out of it completely unhurt but looked warily at her.

She reassured them saying "Do not worry I am Selena Queen of the Mermaids I have come to help you".

The three of them looked at each other slowly getting to their feet.

The man spoke first saying "We have been prisoners in this mirror for weeks. Both my wife and I are only brought out to teach Gledwyn's thoroughly unpleasant child. My name is Max and this is my wife Christine Rump. And the lady with us is Lucella she is a psychic kidnapped from St Lucia many years ago. She has to predict the future for Gledwyn. If she gets its wrong she gets punished". With that Lucella started to cry.

Trying to stop her crying Selena said to her "Dry your tears "said Selena "You are all free. The war against the witches has nearly been won. I have many soldiers. More allies are arriving".

She then asked "Where are you from"?

The woman replied "We are from St Lucia also we were kidnapped and all our pupils were taken... We have a son but do not know what has happened to him". Her voice wavered "We do not know if he is alive. The voice choked back tears. Lucella says he is but you get false hopes. We do not know if we will ever see him again. He could be anywhere, or something worse".

Lucella broke into the conversation and said she was convinced Christine's son was alive.

"Where are the children from the school house? Asked Selena.

The younger woman replied "She has kept them for Larissa as pets... They are trapped in dormitories, and are brought out to play with Larissa. We are allowed to teach them but only because it makes them more interesting if they are educated. Thankfully, nothing worse has happened. We have been worrying what would happen when Larissa got bored with them".

Saros arrived in the doorway of the bedroom. He was swiftly introduced... The rescued prisoners were amazed at the size of the huge dog.

Seeing their fear he smiled at them but it frightened them even more. He had an unfortunate razor teeth which when he smiled made him look more menacing.

"Saros can you and two of my men take these people to safety? I have a feeling there is someone who may be wanting to meet them" said Selena giving a gentle smile." "Madam what about you?" asked Saros.

"Do not worry about me the men I have with me will be fine. Minerus will be joining me shortly".

"Thank you" said Christine grabbing Selina's hand.

"You will be safe with Saros. He is a remarkable soldier" said Selena.

Saros, who for once in his life was lost for words, muttered under his breath what appeared to be the words "Thank you madam". He quickly left the room embarrassed with Christine, Max and Lucella.

Selena went into the next room attached to the bedroom. It was very dark, and unlit. Selena with her wand produced a flying ball of light which lit up the whole room. It was similar shape to the other room except unadorned.

Max, Lucella and Christine followed Saros but he walked so quickly out of the room. It was difficult to keep up with him. Christine, in her haste to keep up had half tripped. Looking down she saw a tiny black kitten at her feet.

Picking the warm wriggling mass of fur she said to herself. "Poor little thing" and stroked it, carrying it in her arms out of the room.

"Isn't that strange," said Christine to Max. "This is the first cat I have ever seen in the tower. Gledwyn must have brought it in recently." The tiny black animal nuzzled her, burrowing itself into her chest. Its emerald eyes gleaming.

The soldiers searched the whole of the tower but Gledwyn was nowhere to be found. It was if she had disappeared into thin air.

Searching the other bedroom Selena had found a similar mirror on the dressing table. Looking into it she saw children in what looked like small dormitories. Selena broke the spell. The children slowly came out of the mirror one by one. Then flew down onto the ground. Looking at her they all huddled up together frightened, but she spoke to them with such tenderness they relaxed.

"You are safe. We have your teachers Max and Christine we will take them to you".

The children all attempted to talk at once, but none of the sentences made any sense. Selena spoke to each child and reassured them.

Speaking to a group of her soldiers she said "Take these children to Max, and Christine and guard them with your lives. Make sure they all go in the large dining room. There is food in the cupboards make sure they have food and water". The soldiers obeyed and the children followed them.

As they went out of the room Selena said to one of her soldiers "Their families must be somewhere. Look under floors, check walls they may be rooms behind them where she has kept them as prisoners. No matter how small rooms are search them. She would have been ready to use them for the Feast of Molina".

A deep voice on the landing could now be heard. Very distinct it was Ethan. He informed Selena that some warlocks had shown him where more people were held captive. She told him to take them to the dining hall. Then Larissa's bedroom was searched. It was the largest room filled with odd looking puppets and toys. Rows upon rows of rail of dresses hung in a walk in wardrobe near her bed. On the floor were shoes of every colour. Some far too big for her.

Selena scanned the room. There was nothing. Seeing a small toad hopping round the room. She looked at it carefully, and a thought filled her head, Checking it she reassured herself .It was not a shape shifter.

She shouted to her soldiers "She may have changed shape and transformed into a small animal - bring any animals to me. Tell Minerus".

Her hair knocked a small hand mirror with a wolf's head on it the ground. Picking it up, she placed it back on Larissa' bedside table.

In the dining room mer children and school children met their parents, and aunts, and uncles. There was a lot of tears.
Tia and Christopher were reunited with their parents. Christopher was lifted high in the air by his father, Tia holding her mother's hand very tightly. Phoebe looked sadly on. Tia

noticing this introduced Phoebe to them. Phoebe was tall, and fair with straight long blonde hair. Her face was covered in freckles lit up with sparkling light grey eyes. They hugged her as if she were their own.

Max and Christine came up and started speaking to Phoebe, more children from Stevie's school came up. Christine had started compiling lists of people in the hall. All the school children were there. But Winnie was still missing.

Ethan and Saros came into the hall. Saro's huge frame blocking anyone standing beside him. For some reason Christine was drawn to the dog soldiers. It was as if it was sixth sense. Saros finally moved, and Christine could see who was in shadow beside him.

Overcome with emotion she just stared not daring to believe what she was seeing. Max turned round to speak to his wife. Followed her gaze and he too looked dumbly across at the figure. Stevie stopped speaking to Ethan. He had a strange feeling in his heart.

The hall was darkly lit with candles but he knew even without looking that someone was watching him. Looking across at this person he found himself looking into Christine hazel's eyes. His whole body felt light, in a dreamlike slumber he began to run in her direction. Running across the hall he fell into his mother's arms. His father Max clamped his arms round his son as Stevie started to cry.

Ethan looking across knew at once who these people were. Smiling at Saros they witnessed the emotional scene, but Saros looked away finding it difficult to deal with.

In the meantime Fergal and Bruce were having a great time tucking into food they had found from the vast pantries.

Bruce already had his face covered in butter, but was loving every minute of it. Rufus the golden eagle had joined the two.

Horobin had been found in a cellar. The witches had covered him in spices ready for cooking. He stank. Saros had poured water over him to get rid of the smell much to his annoyance. Dripping wet, and moaning he had come into the great hall. Seeing food he soon forgot about being wet. He joined Bruce and Fergal and Rufus. The eagle was also too busy to speak to anyone. His sharp beak ripping up pieces of ham. All could be heard was the sound of them guzzling their food.

Stevie and his parents walked up. Stevie introduced his friends to them. Just as he was about to speak Lucella came up and Christine introduced her. .

"These are my two best friends Fergal and Bruce". The pair beamed at Christine, Max and Lucella.

Stevie told his parents about Andrina, and the sea pirates, and the snakes. His parents horrified were only thankful he had managed to stay safe.

Looking back at his parents Stevie was shocked how they had aged. His father's hair a dark brown was now almost white. His mother was now very thin. Worry lines were etched on their foreheads. Their faces were pasty white. No hint of the glistening golden skin they once had. Once they were back home Stevie promised to himself he would spoil them and get them back to their old selves.

Stevie told his parents more stories about Andrina, and the crooked little house. Lucella told him she was Andrina's sister. He was amazed how alike they were. Lucella was just looking forward to seeing her family again. She hated the Sea Witches for what they had done to her and her family.

"I hope they catch Gledwyn and she is brought to trial" she said angrily. "I have nothing but hatred for her.

"Selena will find her "said Christine "She has so much strength. Gledwyn will be brought to justice".

"I just hope it's soon" said Fergal "It is worrying knowing she could be around here".

"When we get back to St Lucia" said Stevie swiftly changing the subject as he could see Lucella was getting distressed he said. "Will you be going to live with Andrina?"

"Good heavens no-"said Lucella. "That untidy heap that's called a house" she said laughing adding "I have my own house. If it's still there on the Island. Why do you ask"?

"I just wondered she will be so excited when she sees you "said Stevie. "And I wondered Dad if Bruce and Fergal could live with us?"

Bruce and Fergal were stunned by their friend and Fergal embarrassed said "Stevie?"

Max answered "We will have our work cut out when we get back. We will have no problem with you staying with us. But you will have to help us build the orphanage and school house. It will take a lot of your time."

Both Max and Christine patted Fergal and Bruce on the shoulders.

"Of course you can boys" said Christine warmly. They both smiled at Bruce and Fergal. "Ethan has given us some gold the Sea Witches had amassed. Selena wanted it to go towards building a home for the orphans".

Bruce broke into the conversation "Me and him" he said pointing at Fergal "Living together". He put his paws up to his face in mock horror making everyone laugh.

"You will have to learn to be tidier" said Fergal solemnly. His wide mouth twitching into a smile.

Bruce folded his paws "I might be able to do that but let's face it. We make a great team. Mrs Rump" he said "Think of the food we will make you. We will be famous on the island for our cuisine". Bruce's eyes widened "Y'Know we could be famous". But I don't think we could have got through all this without you Stevie".

Stevie replied "We helped each other. In a way you are like the brothers I never had. Both of you living with us is my way of keeping my best friends near me. .After all we have been through I could not bear to not see you guys again. Mum Dad you will love them both".

Christine replied" I am sure we will. But it will be just nice to get go back home and have things go back to normal. You, Stevie I will not let out of my sight. I have lost you once. I will not let that happen again. Also, you have a month's school work to catch up on". She stroked his hair as Stevie groaned, Bruce and Fergal smiled at each other.

"As for you two" she said pointing at Bruce and Fergal laughing "I think a few school lessons will be in order for the pair of you too".

"What's that noise? Fergal broke into the conversation straining to hear something. Everyone looked puzzled. The noise got louder, and now everyone could now hear. It was a faint mewing.

Christine said amused "Oh it's my little kitten I found her upstairs. We will take her back home when we go". Everyone gushed over the little black kitten with its vivid green eyes.

Well, apart from Bruce. He would not stroke it. Stevie and Fergal could not understand why. Even his tabby tail had gone thick, and bushy. He then accidentally hissed at it, which made the tiny creature burrow itself timidly into Christine's pocket.

"I am so sorry" said Bruce apologetically. "I don't know why I am doing this. I normally love kittens. Why my tail has shot up like that is beyond me".

"This is not like you" said Fergal remembering how kind Bruce had been to a family of abandoned kittens he had found near the docks...

"Maybe I am just not used to cats anymore after being underwater" sniffed Bruce.

Stevie and Fergal raised their eyebrows at each other. Bruce could be so odd sometimes.

In the middle of the hall Minerus was now talking to Selena "She seems to have completely disappeared. It's baffling. One thing we know for sure she will come for Larissa before she escapes".

"We will place a guard on Larissa" said Selena. They both made their way to where Larissa was. She was in her bedroom and had just woken up. At first she had shouted, and screamed. Finally tears of rage because she hadn't managed to get her own way.

Seeing Selena Larissa smiled in a childlike fashion. This didn't work with Selena.

"Where is your mother Larissa"?

The child looked at Selena with cold eyes. Ignored her, and started playing with the ties on her blue pinafore dress.

"I don't know. Maybe you should ask her if you can find her that is". The girl then proceeded to sing to herself rocking back and forth in a very irritating way.

"Why don't we try the truth drug on her"? Asked Minerus.

"It's too dangerous because she is still very young" said Selena replying to Minerus. "We will keep her locked in her bedroom. I will make sure the magic shield is round the room so she cannot escape".

Both Selena went out of the room beckoning more soldiers to guard it. They split up again Minerus went down one long corridor. Selena decided to go back to the bedroom of Gledwyn.

One of the soldiers half opened the door guarding Larissa as a precaution. "Nothing can get through with the force field. Best we keep it half open so we can check on her". He said to his colleague.

While he was saying this a black ball of fluff dodged through his legs. Trying to stop it, it bounced off the force field. He picked up a dazed kitten.

"A kitten but how did it get here"? Examining the little animal he said. "It's not hurt. Where on earth did that shoot out from?

Larissa hearing the commotion looked in the direction of the door, seeing the kitten smiled. "Oh let me play with it please" she shouted endearingly across to the soldiers.

"Sorry can't do "said one of them. "Our heads would roll if we brought it in. We have strict instructions nothing is allowed in your room. Anyway, we couldn't do it even if we wanted to.

There is a force field round your room". The force field gave off a slight blue glare round the room.

The soldier pointed at it to Larissa and said. "Never mind child you have plenty of toys. Play with them instead". While he was saying this to her the kitten he had been holding scratched him. He shouted in pain. It gave him a deep gash "Ouch" he shouted dropping the struggling kitten.

"Serves you right" said Larissa smirking nastily.

The kitten ran off, and climbed up the steps further up into the tower. It was amazingly fast. The soldier shrugged to his friend. A kitten was hardly a threat he thought.

In the hall Christine realising she had lost the kitten went round searching for it.

"How could it have escaped? I never even felt it leave my pocket".

Stevie tried to help look for it, but there was now so many people now in the hall it was an impossible task.

"Don't worry mum we will find it" he said to her. "But it will be like looking for a needle in a haystack. The tower has so many places it could be in"

His mother replied "Oh dear I just hope the poor creature hasn't been hurt".

Selena was convinced Gladwin was near, and searched again round Gledwyns bedroom. It was such an oppressive room. She noticed more in the room this time. There was small pictures decorating walls round the room. Some were of ogres. One pictured mermaids caught in nets being swallowed by sea monsters. She looked away from it quickly. Looking across the room there was a walnut blanket box. Opening it she found it full of gold. In it was gold and silver snuff boxes, belts, coins, even a jewelled sword and muskets. There was boxes under the bed filled with brocade slippers, and embroidered bags, and a green silk gown. In cupboards she found more dresses in bags, pearl earrings in boxes, and ruby rings.

Selena stopped rummaging through the plunder as there was a strong smell now in the room. The smell was like damp mushrooms .It wasn't pleasant. It made Selena cough. White powder floated about her eyes she began to feel very dizzy. She started to hallucinate imagining creatures coming out of the pictures. Then it felt as if she was falling.

She then realised what had happened.

"I have been drugged" she murmured but there was nothing she could do.

Chapter Fourteen

There was nobody else was in the room to help Selena. The soldiers were in other rooms. She started to fall on the bed, sinking into the covers. She tried to recite rhymes to herself to keep herself awake. Her wand had fallen from her robe when she fell, and went under the bed. The war against the witches had sapped Selena's strength. She lay on the bed, and started to fall asleep, hearing a thud on the bed.

Half opening her eyes she saw a tiny black kitten coming towards her. She stretched out her hand, and stroked the silky black coat. Selena started to fall in and out of strange dreams. As she stroked the kitten. It's back appeared to be getting longer.

"How could that be"? She thought her brain not making sense of it.

The kittens purring was getting louder, and louder.

There was now a thoroughly unpleasant smell emulating from the bed. It smelt like rotten eggs.

Finally managing to half open her eyes, she gazed into the emerald green eyes of an enormous black panther. The smell was its fetid breath.

"Gledwyn" she whispered. The cat's eyes shone looking highly amused at her distress. The animal then cocked its large head to one side to listen her. It was if it was playing a cruel game with her. It proceeded to lick her arm, but the coarse tongue started to shred her skin and Selena shouted out in pain.

It was getting nearer to her chest, fighting the tiredness, Selena turned her body rolling it three times over until she fell off the bed. She was now on the opposite side of the bed from the panther.

The creature snarled, and attempted to pounce on her. Selena pushed herself half under the bed so the panther could not get to her. It stretched its large paws under the bed trying to grab at her. Her drowsiness meant that she would not be able to fight it off much longer. Selena's wand had slid on the ground and had gone further under the bed. It was too far under the bed to reach it.

Selena shouted breathlessly at the panther "Fight like a warrior Gledwyn and not a coward".

The animal bristled, and shrank its body so it could get further under the bed towards her, it's hind legs much longer than its front legs as it moved. Just as it was about to drag her out from the bed there was a white flash of lightening in the room. This was followed by more flashes going off in zig zag directions. It was an amazing scene. The panther was suddenly lifted into the air, and then fell to the floor motionless.

Selena looked across the room. Minerus was half in the room. He continued aiming his wand at the panther until he had created a thin blue line round it. The animal tried to get out of its trap but to no avail. Minerus then put up a force field so it couldn't escape.

The panther started to transform, and screamed in rage. Human features appeared.

Selena looked into Gledwyn's green face. It was trademark thin with a long pointed chin. Her eyes were to at first unemotional .However, looking closer you could fury in them. Pure evil shone through her as she began screaming at Minerus.

"You will regret this Minerus. I will kill you, and all your family. No-one will be left living. That is a promise make no mistake" .She spat the words out screeching again this time almost incoherent. It was frightening listening to her.

She put her head back, and opened her mouth and gave an animal like a roar. Then charged at the blue line but it was to no avail she was stuck firmly behind it. The whole room shook as she shrieked... She then stopped suddenly gazing at Minerus, but he avoided looking directly at her and went to help Selena.

The deep scrap marks on Selena were starting to bleed, and he placed his hand over them. The wounds disappeared. Looking into her face he touched her forehead, and mumbled some words. Selena's tiredness vanished, and she was now wide awake.

Gledwyns magic wand attempted to run away but Selena went back under the bed, grabbed her own wand from under the bed and stopped it in its tracks. It crumpled up in a heap. She uttered some words as she destroyed it into tiny black pieces.

"We had to destroy the wand" she said to Minerus. "In Glewyns case. One who is pure evil will never change. Her wand would have been the same".

Gaining her composure, and her head much clearer she added "Thank you. You are a good friend. I think I may have been drugged. There was a white powder floating above me when I went into the room".

Miners replied "I think there was a drug in the powder in the room. Gledwyn knew if she made you weak she could then be able to kill you".

Gledwyn hearing this muttered further curses at the pair.

Minerus getting bored with all the cussing shouted some words at her. There was now complete silence from her.

"What did you do"? Selena was amused.

"I did what should have been done a long time ago I took away her voice. It's a temporary measure. It ensures we don't have to listen to her foul mouth. She will need to save her voice when she appears in the Supreme Power Court of Justice" said Minerus solemnly.

Gledwyn opened her mouth to shout but no words came out. She gestured at them wildly, but they ignored her, and turned their backs on her.

Ethan and soldiers had now appeared behind Minerus and Ethan asked "What happens at the Court".

He replied "She will be tried fairly along those who have been in allegiance with her. There will be a judge, and jury and witnesses. If she is found guilty. Which I am sure she will be she will be sent to the Wailing Planet. She will never be able to return back here. A spell is cast there that that can never be broken. There is but one secret code. Once it is spoken. The word is immediately destroyed, and can never be repeated."

The Wailing Planet was a huge red planet near Mars. There was no escape. The magic was designed by the Court of Magic so they had made sure of this.

"And Larissa"? Enquired Ethan.

Minerus answered back "Larissa - she will be sent to a special correction school, but holidays will stay with one of the teachers. It will be a change of life for her. She has been brainwashed by her mother. It will take a long time for her to accept that her mother's deeds have been wrong".

"Let's hope it works "said Ethan. He was not convinced about Larissa. In his mind she had the same mind of her mother and could be trouble in the future. He did not comment further. Instead, decided to inspect the rest of the tower with the soldiers. They checked it from head to foot. There was no more secret rooms.

Chapter Fifteen

Animals, and humans, and mer folk had now all been rescued. The human children were now with Christine and Max. They would be travelling back with them. Everyone would have to help rebuilding the school house, the school teachers home, and new orphanage. Make shift shelters would have to be put up in the meantime. With the help of Minerus some magic would be done to get the job done more quickly. He could not create an orphanage. But could help build it.

"I want everyone to gather in the Hall" commanded Selena.

Her soldiers nodded. Everyone followed her into the hall. She stood at the witches alter, and everyone began to cheer. Beckoning them with her hands to stop the noise. It quickly died down.

"Friends" she shouted "We are now free of Gledwyn and her followers. But there is work to be done. People need to be helped. They have lost loved ones. We should all help them. Anyone without a home should be given shelter. This is a new era we help each other and work together. The days of the Gledwyn are over the homes she has destroyed we must rebuild. Anyone who has been robbed we will help. We have found treasure chests. Some of the monies are going towards building an orphanage at Soufriere. Other monies will be to be for repairs to houses that have been burnt. We also need monies to build our soldiers up. If we do not build up our defences more Sea Witches will try and take over again.

Our friend Minerus and his warlocks will help with the rebuilding of homes. Ethan and Saros" she said pointing at them "Will help lead our armies, Louisa is my second in command, and will help me and will act as an ambassador."

Louisa had arrived on a ship at the tower and stood with the people at the back of the hall. She walked down the hall and stood beside Selena. Minerus joined her. There was more clapping.

"I would like to thank three more brave souls Stevie, Fergal and Bruce stand up please ". The trio stood up. "These three "shouted Selena to the crowd "Freed me. I owe them a great deal. Come here boys" Fergal, Stevie and Bruce joined her on the platform.

Selena placed gold amulets round their necks. "We owe you a great debt and we thank you".

The three shyly looked up as the crowd clapped. Even the magpies who had been captured clucked approvingly. They had been given their freedom. Max and Christine could only look in amazement at their brave son. He had matured greatly in that month. Magic wands floated around above high up into the ceiling chattering to each other. They were no longer frightened to speak to each other.

Seeing Meena, Stevie and Bruce and Fergal spoke to her. The little wand full of excitement told them she would stay with Ethan. She said she felt he would need her, as she spoke her tiny eyes looked adoring at her hero.

"We will now give a minutes silence to those we have lost" said Selena.

Bruce put his head down with everyone else. Tears falling down his cheeks thinking about his Auntie Lucy. She had not been at the tower as he had hoped. Fergal also with his own thoughts thinking about Connor, and the other brave cormorants who had been captured lost their lives in the tower.

After the minutes silence everyone came out of the hall still very quiet. Coming out into the fresh sea breeze it was difficult for the freed prisoners. They had never seen the sun for a month. The tower had been engulfed in black clouds. Now the blazing sun shone brightly. The sky and turquoise sea was now full of colour. Monk seals that would normally never have set foot on Glendowwer gathered round the rocks in groups. The whole island was filled with noise. Minerus had placed a spell on the sand. The sand witches had been banished to another planet. But there was no sign of the legendary zombies.

"Maybe there never was any" said Fergal.

"Let's hope that's the case" said Christine. "It would be horrible to think there had been people trapped here and that Gledwyn had taken their souls".

The Dog Solders had all now gathered together. Saros and Ethan came up to Stevie and Fergal and Bruce "Well done boys" said Ethan patting their backs, but his sheer strength in his arms sent them nearly rolling over.

All Saros said was "I still can't believe you three released Selena". His huge dark head shook from side to side still in disbelief. Unable to comprehend it, and probably never would.

Mer folk were now going back to the ocean. Tia raced up to Ethan attempting to tickle him, but his huge paw grabbed her tiny hand before she could do so. Her family beside her.

Ethan looked down at her "I will miss you little one" he said affectionately."

"I won't be far "said Tia gaily replying "I know your ship so I will look out for you".

Ethan bent his huge head as she gave him a kiss on the cheek. His eyes glinted. The little mermaid had charmed his stone heart.

Her legs were slowly transforming into a silver tail. The sucking noise started. Looking around in embarrassment, she needn't have been as all the mer folk were slowly going through the same transformation.

"Good Bye" said Tia to Fergal, Bruce and Stevie.

"Come and see us "said Christine.

"I will" said Tia. Turning to Phoebe she hugged her. "Please keep in touch with me Phoebe".

"I will" said Phoebe". With that Tia, Christopher and her family waded into the water. As they got deeper into the water, all you could see was a swish of silver tails, which you would if you didn't know would mistake for a group of seals.

Christine put her arms round Phoebe sensing her distress saying "Don't worry you are safe with us".

"Yes" said Max "You are part of our family now. So remember that when you are carrying bricks to build the house, and it makes you groan". Phoebe smiled.

Lucella appeared in front of them. She was going to travel on the ship with Max, Christine, Phoebe and Stevie and Fergal and Bruce.

"Andrina is going to be so pleased when she sees you" said Stevie.

"I've a feeling" said Lucella "She already knows. Most people would call it a sisters bond". But then she became quite distressed thinking about all that had happened, and how long she had been away.

Stevie swiftly changed the subject. Where's Winnie"? Said Stevie feeling guilty he had not asked before.

"We don't know "said Max "That doesn't mean anything bad has happened to her it. It could mean she may be on another Island being used as a slave. Other Islands are being checked. There may other Sea Witches on them. It will take a long time to go through them all".

Bruce listening to this thought again of his Auntie Lucy. Maybe she too was on an Island. It gave him some hope, but he didn't share his feelings with the others.

Saros and Ethan started to lose interest in the emotional displays round them.

"Come on" said Saros gruffly to everyone "It's time we got on the ship". They did as they were told. They walked down to the beach. Small boats took them out to "The Black Scorpion" and they climbed aboard.

Once they were on board Ethan yelled at the crew "Come on you lazy beggars get going we haven't got all day".

The crew were used to his sharp tone. But he treated them well. They respected him.

Saros, however was another matter they thought. Something to be reckoned with. The ship gave a jolt, and started to slowly move.

Stevie and Fergal and Bruce watched the black tower slowly disappeared into a black speck...

"What will happen to the Black Tower"?

Ethan replied to Stevie, "Selena is going to have it used as a watch tower. Some soldiers will remain there on guard. We have heard news that the English have joined up with her. They will patrol the seas. The Sea Witches made a lot of enemies. They thought they were too powerful. "

Breaking into the conversation which made Ethan sigh. Bruce said puzzled "I can smell food but it smells horrible" although secretly pleased the new cook wasn't very good.

"That is our cook don't be so rude. If you are hungry go in the kitchen" said Ethan. "You will all have to feed yourselves".

Bruce and Fergal charged ahead of everyone else. They knew the kitchen.

"Ready to help with the cooking" said Fergal

"You bet "replied Bruce "And maybe help myself in the process".

The cook a walrus was not happy with the newcomers, barging their way in.

"Don't worry" said Fergal "We only want to help you".

Soon Fergal and Bruce were preparing an enormous feast. Herbert the Walrus along with his assistant a parrot called Jake reluctantly helped. Fergal made his special goat curry, and Kingfish soup. Bruce made miniature meat pies, crimping the edges with one side of his left claw. Herbert not to be outdone prepared his own pineapple cake layered with cream, and jellied fruits.

"Well I think it was nice of the Sea Witches to leave us all this food" said Fergal. The soldiers had removed food that was for the Feast of Molina. They were placed in baskets for ships setting sail.

"Well they checked it thoroughly and I certainly would not have eaten any of the sandwiches they had made. God knows what was in them" said Stevie coming in.

"Phoebe, said Stevie seeing her in the doorway looking lost "Do you want to help. I am going to lay the dining room table"?

"Sure anything to get near the food" she replied laughing.

As they were going into the dining room Meena appeared "Need some help?" she said hovering above them.

"Please "they both said in unison. Meena made a beautifully white damask tablecloth appear out of nowhere. It flew across the table, then, straightened itself out. Candlesticks, and bread, and fruit appeared in bowls across the table. Flagons of wine, and a huge jug of water appeared.

"Don't do anything else Meena "said Stevie "Bruce and Fergal and Herbert are preparing all the food".

"As you wish"" she replied and flew away whistling a tune to herself.

Christine coming into the dining room and was impressed. "Stevie, Phoebe this looks great "she looked further at the table, and all its finery. Amazed at her son. Stevie and Phoebe gave each other a knowing look and didn't say anything.

Then Stevie had a horrible thought "Mum, just a warning when we sit down to eat the Dog Pirates do not have the best table manners. Don't be shocked".

His mother replied "Their eating can't be any worse than watching Gledwyn enjoying a meal". She pulled a wry face at some unpleasant memory she had of her.

Outside Ethan and Saros were talking. The soldiers had not located the other McCarthy twin.

"He will probably hide out on another Island but his brother Seth will go to trial" said Ethan.

Saros in reply said "Why don't we when we drop off these passengers at Soufriere see if we can find out where he has gone? He will lie low. His trademark white fur coat may stand out. We might catch him that way. Or, someone might inform on him. ".

"That's a good idea let us and hope he is found sooner rather than later "said Ethan.

"When will Minerus come to Soufriere" asked Max joining them on deck.

Ethan said "After the trial of Gledwyn. He will go with Selena to the Crown Court of Justice. Once it's settled he will no doubt come to the Island and overseer the building of the orphanage".

Back in the kitchen Bruce, Stevie and Fergal had finished cooking. Everything had to be made in huge quantities. There was so many people, and children on the ship there had to be three sittings for dinner.

After dinner Stevie, Bruce and Fergal walked on to the deck, and looked out at the turquoise sea. A flock of red, and green parrots were flying towards Soufriere. They were finally going back to Stevie's home. The three continued looking out to sea. No words were spoken but there was a bond between the three friends which would never be broken.

In the Black Tower Larissa was packing to go to the boarding school. Eleanor one of the mermaids, and a group of soldiers helped her place things in boxes.

"Can I carry my mirror in my satchel?" asked Larissa.

"Won't it break?" said Eleanor

"Oh no "said Larissa "It's a very strong mirror. I'll be very careful. My mother gave it to me" said Larissa looking at her with her eyes full of tears, then she started to sniff.

Eleanor feeling sorry for the little girl, handed her a handkerchief "Of course you can take the mirror dear wipe your eyes. Don't be sad. Look there is some parchment paper. Use that to wrap it up, so it is well protected".

Larissa grabbed Eleanor's hand, and said thank you. Eleanor then became preoccupied with packing Larissa's many clothes.

Larissa carefully wrapped the silver hand mirror, with its heavily engraved wolf's head in the heavy parchment paper. Then, firmly sealed up with the paper, she placed it in her brown leather satchel.

A crooked smile formed on her lips. In the darkness of the leather bag a cruel yellow eyed face looked out of the mirror. The face was that of the one who started the first War of the

Mermaids. The old woman had a huge beak of a nose, and thin black lips. Her grey hair fanned out round her face in knotted spirals. Looking closer you would see they were really small red eyed adders twisted round her head.

Larissa's great grandmother had a new pupil to teach in the ways of the sea witches, just as she had taught her daughter and Gledwyn all those years ago.

The End

19179969R00114

Printed in Great Britain
by Amazon